"I don't want to

"Perhaps not…tonight," Luc insisted silkily.

"Not *any* night!"

"Brave words, Ana."

Ana wanted to rail against him, hating the power he possessed and her inability to retaliate. She was caught in a web, tied to him by the child they'd conceived, and held there by family loyalty.

"*Go to hell*, Luc," she said bitterly as he drew level.

Luc paused and caught hold of her chin, tilting it so she had little option but to meet his passionate gaze. "Careful, *pedhaki mou*. I might be tempted to take you there."

Dear Reader,

Flowers signify so many emotions…they're the gift of lovers, friends and family, in times of happiness, joy and sorrow. From the exotic to simple everyday blossoms, their textures, colors and perfumes blend together to bring pleasure to people all around the world.

I have an admiration for those who work in the floral industry, especially the talented florists whose skilled artistry turns varied blooms into beautiful bouquets. My writer's imagination envisaged the lives of two sisters, **Ana** and **Rebekah,** who co-own a florist boutique in one of the trendiest suburbs of Sydney, Australia.

Ana is married to proud, powerful **Luc Dimitriades—** but one year into their marriage, his newly divorced ex-mistress returns, determined to reclaim Luc…

Rebekah is wary of men and determined to avoid falling in love again. But Luc's cousin **Jace Dimitriades** plans to change her mind!

I hope you enjoy getting to know these two sisters, and the gorgeous tycoons who turn their world upside down!

With love

Helen Bianchin

Look out for Rebekah's story
The Greek Bridegroom
Harlequin Presents #2284, on sale in November

Helen Bianchin

A PASSIONATE SURRENDER

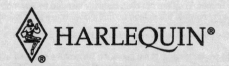

HARLEQUIN®

TORONTO • NEW YORK • LONDON
AMSTERDAM • PARIS • SYDNEY • HAMBURG
STOCKHOLM • ATHENS • TOKYO • MILAN • MADRID
PRAGUE • WARSAW • BUDAPEST • AUCKLAND

For Helga,
friend and talented florist

ISBN 0-373-12279-9

A PASSIONATE SURRENDER

First North American Publication 2002.

Copyright © 2002 by Helen Bianchin.

Visit us at www.eHarlequin.com

Printed in U.S.A.

CHAPTER ONE

'*CRISTOS.*'

The husky imprecation held an angry silkiness as Luc Dimitriades tossed the faxed report down onto his desk.

Detailed surveillance of his wife's movements during the past nine days revealed few surprises, although one caused his eyes to narrow with contemplative suspicion.

Reflex action had him reaching for his cellphone and keying in a series of digits.

'Put me through to Marc Andreas,' he instructed curtly as soon as the receptionist picked up.

'Doctor has a patient with him.'

'It's urgent,' he said without compunction, and identified himself. 'He'll take the call.'

Minutes later he had official confirmation, and his expression hardened as he reached for the inter-office phone.

Clear, concise instructions set his plan in motion, and after replacing the receiver he stood to his feet and crossed to the large plate-glass window.

The city and harbour spread out before him in splendid panorama. Sparkling blue sea, tall office buildings in varying height and design of concrete, steel and glass. Expensive two- and three-level mansions nestled between trees and shrubbery on a carved-out rock-face overlooking the inner harbour.

Small craft moored in safe anchorage dotting inlets and coves. The bustling water-cats and ferries vying with a huge tanker being guided by tugboats into berth. The familiar arch of Sydney's bridge, the distinctive architecture of the opera house.

It was a familiar sight. Yet today he didn't register the view. Nor the expensive furnishings, the genuine art gracing the walls of his luxurious office.

There was no pleasure of the scene evident in his broad, chiselled features, little emotion in his dark brooding gaze as he lapsed into reflective thought.

A brief marriage in his early twenties to his childhood sweetheart had ended tragically with Emma's accidental death mere months after their wedding. Grief-stricken, he'd thrown himself into work, putting in long hours and achieving untold success in the business arena.

Remarriage wasn't on his agenda. He'd loved and lost, and didn't want to lose his heart again. For the past ten years he'd enjoyed a few selective relationships…no commitments, no empty words promising permanence.

Until Ana.

The daughter of one of his executives, she'd often partnered her widowed father to various functions. She was attractive, in her mid-twenties, intelligent and she possessed a delightful sense of humour.

What was more, she wasn't in awe of him, his status or his wealth.

They'd dated a few months, enjoyed each other in bed, and for the first time since Emma's death there was an awareness of his own mortality, his accumulated wealth...the need to share his life with one woman, have children with her, forge a future together.

Who better than Ana in the role of his wife? He cared for her, she was eminently suitable, and he could provide her with an enviable lifestyle.

The wedding had been a low-key affair attended by immediate family, followed by a few weeks in Hawaii, after which they settled easily into day-to-day life.

A year on, the only blight on the horizon was Celine Moore, an ex-mistress, very recently divorced and hell-bent on causing mischief.

Luc's mouth tightened into a grim line as he recalled the few occasions when Celine had deliberately orchestrated a compromising situation. Incidents he'd dealt with with skilled diplomacy and the warning to desist. Something Celine refused to heed, and her persistence became an issue Ana found difficult to condone.

Less than two weeks ago an argument over breakfast had ended badly, and he'd arrived home that evening to discover Ana had packed a bag and taken a flight to the Gold Coast.

The note she'd left him declared a need for a few days away to *think things through.*

Except *a few days* had become nine, and the latter thirty-six hours of which had resulted in unreturned calls from voice-mail and text messages left on her cellphone.

Her father, upon confrontation, swore she wasn't answering *his* messages either, and he had every reason not to lie.

Rebekah, her younger sister and business partner, also disavowed any knowledge of Ana's whereabouts, other than to cite a holiday resort on the Gold Coast, from which enquiries revealed Ana had checked out within a few days of registering.

Hence Luc had no hesitation in engaging the services of a private detective, whose verbal updates were now detailed in a faxed report.

Ana's actions merely confirmed Luc's suspicions. A newly leased apartment and employment weren't conducive to a temporary break.

However, he could deal with that, and numerous scenarios of just *how* he'd deal with it occupied his mind. Foremost of which was the intention to haul her over his shoulder and bring her home.

Something, he decided grimly, he should have done within a day or two of her leaving, instead of allowing her the distance, time and space she'd vowed so desperately to need. Yet she'd done the unexpected by attempting to cover her tracks... without success.

Surely she couldn't believe he'd let her separation bid drag on for long?

The inter-office phone rang, and he crossed to the desk to take the call.

'The pilot is on standby, and your car is out front.'

Smooth efficiency came with a high-priced salary.

'Petros will have a bag packed by the time you reach the house.'

'Thanks.'

An hour later Luc boarded the private jet, sank into one of four plush armchairs, and prepared for take-off.

'Go take a lunch break.'

Ana attached the ribbon, tied a deft bow, utilised the slim edge of the scissors to curl the ribbon ends, then set the bouquet of roses to one side.

It was her third day as an assistant at a florist shop in the trendy suburb of Main Beach. She'd entered the shop on a whim, bought flowers to brighten her newly acquired apartment, and, noticing the owner's harassed expression, she'd jokingly asked if the owner required help, citing her experience as a florist. What she didn't impart was that she co-owned her own business in an upmarket Sydney suburb.

Incredible as it seemed, acquiring a job had been as simple as being in the right place at the right time.

Fate, it seemed, had taken a hand, although eventually she'd have to address her sojourn from Sydney, her marriage.

A hollow laugh escaped her throat as she caught up her shoulder bag and walked out onto the pavement.

It was a beautiful early summer day, the sun was warm, and there was a slight breeze drifting in from the ocean.

The usual lunch crowd filled the many cafés lining Tedder Avenue, and she crossed the street, selected an empty table and sank into a seat.

Efficient service ensured almost immediate attention, and she gave her order, then sipped chilled bottled water as she flipped through the pages of a magazine.

An article caught her eye, and she read the print with genuine interest, only to put it to one side as the waitress delivered a steaming bowl of vegetable risotto. There was also a fresh bread roll, and she picked up a fork and began eating the delectable food.

The chatter from patrons seated at adjoining tables provided a pleasant background, combining with the faint purr of vehicles slowly cruising the main street in search of an elusive parking space.

Expensive cars, wealthy owners who strolled the trendy street to one of several outdoor cafés where *lunch with friends* was more about being *seen* than satisfying a need for food.

Ana liked the ambience, enjoyed being a part of it, and the similarity to equally trendy areas in Sydney didn't escape her.

It was relatively easy to tamp down any longing for the city where she'd been born and raised. Not so easy to dismiss the man she'd married a little more than a year ago.

Luc Dimitriades possessed the height, breadth of shoulder and attractive good looks to turn any woman's head. Add sophisticated charm, an aura of power, and the result was devastating.

Australian-born of Greek parents, he'd chosen academia and entered the field of merchant banking, rising rapidly through the ranks to assume a position that involved directorial decision-making.

Inherited wealth combined with astute business acumen ensured he numbered high among the country's rich and famous.

For Ana, all it had taken was one look at him and the attraction was instant, cataclysmic. Sheer sexual chemistry, potent and electric. Yet it was more than that…much more. He affected her as no man ever had, and she fell deeply, irretrievably in love with him.

It was the reason she accepted his marriage proposal, and she convinced herself it was enough he vowed his fidelity and promised to honour and care for her.

THE CATCH OF THE DECADE one national newspaper had captioned when Luc Dimitriades had taken Ana Stanford as his bride.

Maybe, given time, his affection for her would become love, and a year into the marriage she was content. She had an attentive husband, the sex was to die for, and life had assumed a pleasant routine.

Until Celine, always the temptress, re-entered the scene, newly divorced, and *hunting*…with Luc as her prey.

Subtle destruction, carefully orchestrated to diminish Ana's confidence. The divorcee was very clever in aiming her verbal barbs out of Luc's hearing. Implying an affair, citing dates and times when Luc was absent on business or when he'd extended a business meeting to include dinner with colleagues. Merely excuses given in order to be with Celine.

Doubt and suspicion, coupled with anger and jealousy built over a period of weeks.

Even now, the thought of Celine's recent contretemps made Ana grit her teeth. Despite Luc's denial, where there was smoke, there were embers just waiting to be fanned into flame. And infidelity was something she refused to condone.

Angry words had led to a full-scale argument, and afterwards Ana had simply made a few phone calls, packed a bag and taken the midday flight to the Gold Coast.

Apart from the note she'd left him, her only attempt at contact was a recorded message she'd left on Luc's answer-machine, and she doubted it would appease him for long.

'Ana.'

The voice was all too familiar, its inflexion deep and tinged with a degree of mocking cynicism.

There had been no instinctive sixth sense that might have alerted her to his presence. Nothing to warn of the unexpected.

Ana slowly raised her head and met her husband's steady gaze. Unwanted reaction kicked in, and she banked it down, aware on a base level of the damning effect he had on her senses.

She felt vulnerable, exposed, and way too needy. It wasn't a feeling she coveted, at least not now, not here, when she'd vowed to think with her head, not her heart.

Fat chance. All it took was one look, a few seconds in his presence, and her emotions went every which way but loose!

How was it possible to love, yet hate someone with equal measure?

She could think of any number of reasons to justify the way she felt... Ambivalence, out-of-whack hormones. The desire to hurt, as she hurt.

Why, then, did she possess this crazy urge to feel the sanctuary of his arms and the brush of his mouth on her own? The heat of his body ...

A silent screeching cry rose from somewhere deep inside. *Don't go there.*

Instead, she forced herself to subject him to an analytical appraisal, deliberately noting the broad facial bone structure which lent his features a chiselled look that was enhanced by piercing dark eyes, a firm muscled jaw, and a mouth to die for.

Well-groomed hair as dark as sin grew thick on

his head, and he wore it slightly longer than was currently in vogue.

Attired in a three-piece business suit, deep blue shirt and impeccably knotted silk tie, he exuded an aura of invincible power.

Tall, dark and dangerous was an apt descriptive phrase, she perceived, sensing the ruthlessness hovering just beneath the surface of his control.

'Mind if I join you?'

'What if I say no?'

He offered a faint smile, and wondered if she knew how well he could read her. 'It wasn't a rhetorical question.'

Ana held his gaze. 'Then why ask?'

Luc took the seat opposite, ordered black coffee from a hovering waitress, then focused his attention on his wife.

She looked pale, and she'd lost a few essential kilos from her petite frame. There were faint shadows evident, as if she hadn't been sleeping well, and her eyes were dark with fatigue. Instead of its usual attractive style, her honey-blonde hair was pulled back into a pony-tail.

His silent appraisal irked her unbearably. 'Are you done?' Her voice sounded tense even to her own ears.

He resembled a sleekly powerful predator deceptively at ease. Except his seemingly relaxed façade didn't fool her in the slightest. There wasn't any doubt he'd pounce...merely a matter of *when*.

'No,' Luc intimated as she pushed the bowl of partly eaten food to one side.

'Eat,' Luc bade quietly, and she threw him a baleful glare.

'I've lost my appetite.'

'Order something else.'

She barely resisted the temptation to throw something at him. 'Should I ask how you discovered my whereabouts?'

His gaze didn't waver, and his eyes were cool, fathomless. 'I would have thought the answer self-explanatory.'

'You hired a private detective.' Her voice rose a fraction. 'And had me followed?'

'Did you think I wouldn't?'

Hadn't this scenario haunted her for the past few days? Invading her sleep, unsettling her nerves?

The waitress delivered his coffee, and he requested the bill.

'I'll pay for my own meal.'

He shot her a hard glance. 'Don't be ridiculous.'

She checked her watch. 'What do you want, Luc? I suggest you cut to the chase. I'm due back at work in ten minutes.'

Luc selected a paper tube of sugar and emptied it into his cup. 'No, you're not,' he declared silkily.

Her gaze locked with his. 'What do you mean... *no*?'

'You no longer have a job, and your apartment lease has been terminated.'

She felt as if all the breath had suddenly left her body. Angry consternation darkened her eyes, and faint pink coloured her cheeks. 'You have no right—'

'Yes.' His voice was deadly quiet. 'I do.'

She badly wanted to hit him, and almost did. 'No, you don't,' she reiterated fiercely.

'We can argue this back and forth, but the end result will be the same.'

'If you think I'll calmly go back to Sydney with you,' she began heatedly, 'you can think again!'

His gaze seared hers. 'This afternoon, tonight, tomorrow. It hardly matters when.'

Ana rose to her feet, only to have his hand close over her arm, halting her intention to leave.

Without pausing for thought she picked up the sugar container and hurled it at him, watching with a sense of horrified fascination as he fielded it neatly and replaced it on the table, then calmly gathered up the scattered tubes.

'I intend to file for divorce.' Dear heaven, where had that come from? Until now it had been a hazy choice she'd considered and discounted a hundred times during the sleepless night hours since fleeing Sydney.

His gaze seared hers. 'Divorce isn't an option.'

She stood trapped as the silence stretched between them, a haunting entity that became more significant with every passing second, and there was little she could do but comply as he exerted sufficient pressure to ensure she sank down onto the chair.

'Don't you have something to tell me?' Luc prompted with deceptive mildness, and glimpsed her apprehension before she successfully masked it.

'Go away and leave me alone?' Ana taunted in return.

'Try again.'

A muscle twisted painfully in her stomach, and she barely suppressed the instinct to soothe it with her hand.

He couldn't possibly know. *Could he?* She went suddenly cold at the thought. For the past few weeks she'd alternated between joy and despair.

'I'll make it easy for you,' Luc ventured with deadly softness. 'You're carrying my child.'

'A child that is also *mine*,' Ana said fiercely.

'Ours.' His silky tone sent shivers down her spine. 'I refuse to be relegated to a weekend father, restricted to sharing my son or daughter on a part-time basis.'

'Is that why you came after me? Because I suddenly have something you want?' Her eyes darkened to the deepest sapphire, her anger very real at that precise moment. Yet inside she wanted to weep. For the child she'd conceived. For herself, for wanting the love of a man who she doubted would ever love her.

'I'd rather be a single parent than attempt to raise a child in a household where its father divides his time between its mother and his mistress. How could the child begin to understand values, morals, and integrity?'

'*Mistress?*' His voice was quiet.

Too quiet, she perceived, and suppressed a faint shiver.

'You accuse me of having an affair?'

'Celine—'

'Was someone with whom I shared a brief relationship three, four years ago.'

'According to her, the affair is ongoing.'

'Why would I need a mistress when I have you?'

Remembering their active sex life, the sheer delight they shared in bed, brought a tinge of colour to her cheeks. 'For the hell of it?' she ventured carelessly, adding, 'Because you're insatiable and one woman isn't enough?'

His features hardened and assumed an implacable mask. 'Don't tempt me to say something I might regret.'

'Go back to Sydney, Luc.' She was like a runaway train that couldn't stop. 'There's nothing you can say or do that'll persuade me to return with you.'

'No?'

She sensed the steel beneath the dangerously silky tone, and suppressed an illusory premonition.

'The last time I heard, coercion carries no weight in a court of law.'

He held a trump card, and he had no hesitation in playing it. 'However, embezzlement does.' He paused, watching her expressive features in a bid to assess whether she had any prior knowledge William Stanford had indulged in creative accounting over a six-month time span.

'Excuse me?'

Luc chose his words with care, weighing each for its impact. 'The bank's auditors have discovered a series of discrepancies.'

'How can that involve me?' she queried, genuinely puzzled.

'Indirectly, it does.'

Even a naïve fool could do simple arithmetic, and she considered herself to be neither. 'You're implying my *father* is responsible?' she demanded in disbelief. 'I don't believe you.'

He reached inside his jacket, withdrew a folded document and placed it in front of her. 'A copy of the auditors' report.'

Ana touched the paper hesitantly, then she opened the document and read the report.

It was conclusive and damning, the attached spreadsheet listing each transaction lengthy and detailed.

She felt herself go cold. Embezzlement, theft... they were one and the same, and a punishable crime.

Luc studied her expressive features, witnessed the fleeting emotions, and anticipated her loyalty.

'It was very cleverly done,' he revealed with a degree of cynicism. So much so, it had been missed twice. He wasn't sure which angered him more…the loss of trust in one of his valued executives, or the fact William Stanford had relied on his daughter's connection by marriage to avoid prosecution.

'How long have you known?' Ana queried with a sense of dread, unwilling to examine where this was going, yet desperately afraid her wildest suspicion would be proven true.

'Nine days.'

Coincidentally the time she wrote him a note and took a flight north. Did he think that was the reason she left?

Men of Luc's calibre always had a back-up plan. And this was personal. Very personal.

'What do you want, Luc?'

'No divorce. Our child.' He waited a beat. 'My wife in my home, my bed.'

'Go to hell.'

One eyebrow rose in mockery. 'Not today, *agape mou*.'

Pink coloured her cheekbones and lent her eyes a fiery sparkle. 'You think you can make conditions and have me meekly comply?'

'*Meek* wasn't a descriptive I considered.'

Dear heaven, he was amused. She stood to her feet, gathered her bag and slung the strap over her shoulder, then she turned in the direction of the florist shop, aware that Luc fell into step at her side.

'I intend explaining to the letting agent and my

employer that you're a presumptuous, arrogant bastard with no right to dictate my life.'

'And your father will go to jail.'

Her step faltered as she threw him a look that would have felled a lesser man. 'How come you get to make the rules?'

'Because I can.'

'And I get to choose whether to resume my marriage to you, in return for no charges laid against my father.' There was no doubt Luc viewed this as just another business proposition. Well, damn him. She'd do the same. 'What of restitution?'

'It will be taken care of.'

'And his job?'

'Already terminated.'

She was dying inside, inch by inch. 'His references?' she pursued tightly.

'I have a duty of disclosure.'

Something that would make it almost impossible for her father to gain a similar position anywhere in Sydney…possibly even the country.

'I'll think about it,' Ana conceded, endeavouring to ignore the prickle of apprehension steadily creating havoc with her nervous system.

His eyes were hard, their expression implacable. 'You have an hour.'

She closed her eyes, then opened them again, and released the breath she'd unconsciously held for several seconds.

'Are you this diabolically relentless in the business

arena?' Stupid question, she mentally castigated. His steel-willed determination and ruthless decision-making had earned him a reputation as one of the city's most feared negotiators.

His silence sent an icy chill feathering the length of her spine, and she cursed him afresh.

They reached the florist shop, and she turned towards him, her eyes gleaming with hidden anger as she met and held his dark gaze.

'There are a few conditions.'

His gaze hardened, and he resisted the urge to shake her within an inch of her life. 'You're hardly in a position to stipulate conditions.'

Did he know how much she hurt? Just looking at him caused her physical pain, remembering the hopes and dreams she'd held, only to have them shatter one by one.

She began counting off the fingers of one hand. 'I want your word you won't attempt to deny me my child once it's born.'

Something moved in his eyes, an emotion she didn't care to define. 'Granted.'

'Your fidelity.'

'You've had that since day one.'

She looked at him long and hard, then lifted an eyebrow in silent query. 'Not according to Celine.'

'Naturally, you choose to believe her over me.' His dry tones held a damning cynicism she chose to ignore.

'There's just one more thing,' she pursued.

It was impossible to tell much from his expression, and she didn't even try.

'And that is?'

'I want it all in writing and legally notarised before I give you my answer.'

As an exit line it took some beating, and she didn't look back as she stepped into the florist shop.

'I wasn't expecting you.'

Stiff formality replaced a former easy friendliness, and Ana silently cursed Luc afresh.

'I'm responsible for my own decisions,' she assured evenly. Her gaze was steady as the silence stretched into seemingly long seconds before the shop's owner offered,

'He doesn't look the type of man who'd take *no* for an answer.'

Wasn't that the truth! 'I can give you this afternoon, if that's OK?'

'I've already put in a call to the employment agency.'

What else did she expect?

'Are you going to return to Sydney with him?'

'Possibly.' Ana deposited her bag out back, and checked the order book, then she set to work.

Concentration was the key, but all too frequently it wavered as she examined one scheme after another, only to discard each of them. Where could she go that Luc wouldn't find her?

A faint shiver raised the fine hairs on the back of her neck. If he'd had a private investigator following her every move, it was feasible the man was still on duty. It gave her a creepy feeling, and made her incredibly angry.

Luc had played the game with consummate skill in presenting her with a *coup de grâce*.

But the game had only just begun, and she intended to play by the rules...her own.

CHAPTER TWO

How long would it take Luc to consult a lawyer and have the requested paperwork completed? With his influence and connections, she doubted he'd have a problem.

The shop was busy, there were several phone orders, and people walked in off the street to select purchases. Single roses, bouquets, cut flowers for a special hospital visit…the requests were numerous and varied.

She was in the middle of assembling decorative Cellophane and gathering baby's breath when the door buzzer sounded for the umpteenth time. She automatically glanced up from her task to greet the new customer, and saw Luc observing her actions.

There was an element of formidability existent, a sense of purpose that was daunting, and Ana was conscious of an elevated sense of nervous tension.

Her hands paused as her gaze locked with his, then she bent her head and focused on fashioning pink and white carnations into an elaborate spray.

Ribbon completed the bouquet, and she attached the completed card, the instruction slip, then transferred it to the delivery table.

'Are you done?' Luc queried silkily, his gaze

caught by a tendril of hair that had worked its way loose from her pony-tail, and he restrained the urge to sweep it back behind her ear.

She shot him a cool glance. 'I finish at six.'

The atmosphere in the room seemed suddenly charged, and she could almost feel the latent electricity apparent.

His eyes narrowed with a chilling bleakness. 'You can do better than that.'

'We're busy.' Hot damn, she was so polite it was almost comical. She made a thing of checking the time. 'I'm sure you can manage to fill in a few hours.'

He could, easily. However, he didn't feel inclined to pander to her deliberate manipulation. 'One hour, Ana,' he warned in a voice that was deadly soft.

'Are you mad?' the older woman queried the instant Luc left the shop.

'Certifiably,' Ana agreed imperturbably.

'Gutsy, too. I admire that in a woman.'

She was a fool to think she could best him. Except she was damned if she'd allow him to set down terms and expect her to abide by every one of them without a fight.

'I'm going to be sorry to lose you, honey. We were just beginning to get along.'

'I could be back,' Ana said with humour, and heard the other woman's laughter.

'I doubt he'll let you get away again. Now, why don't you go finish up? I can manage the rest.' Her eyes twinkled with mischief. 'Besides, I'm not averse to a woman stirring a man up a bit.'

Leave, and not be here when Luc returned? 'You're wicked.'

'Good luck, honey. If you're ever back up this way again, call in and say hello.' She withdrew an envelope from her pocket. 'Your pay.'

'Keep it in lieu of notice.'

'Some would. I won't. Now go.'

It took five minutes to walk to her apartment, and once inside she headed straight for the kitchen, extracted bottled water from the refrigerator, uncapped the lid and drank until her thirst was quenched, then she made for the bedroom, stripped off her clothes and hit the shower.

She washed her hair, then dressed in jeans and a singlet top, opted to forgo make-up and piled her damp hair into a loose knot atop her head.

Packing would probably be a good move, but somehow achieving it indicated her imminent return to Sydney, and sheer stubbornness ensured she put off such a task for as long as possible. Besides, how long did it take to empty a few clothes and possessions into a travel-bag?

It was five when the intercom buzzed, and Ana's stomach did a quick somersault at the sound. It had to be Luc. No one else knew her address.

She cleared him through security into the main lobby, and then waited for the lift to reach her designated floor.

Her doorbell rang all too soon, and she took a calming breath as she crossed the lounge.

He stood looming large in the aperture, dark and vaguely threatening. He'd removed his jacket and hooked it over one shoulder, his tie was missing, he'd loosened the top few buttons of his shirt and folded the cuffs back from each wrist. It lent him a casual air that was belied by his deliberately enigmatic expression.

Ana met his gaze with fearless disregard, and ignored the increased thud of her heartbeat. 'I refuse to be treated like a runaway child on the verge of being dragged home by its parent.'

He didn't move so much as a muscle. 'Whatever happened to *hello*?'

She drew in a deep breath, then released it slowly. 'You want *polite*?'

One eyebrow assumed a mocking slant. 'Shall we start over?' Luc countered coolly.

'Not in this lifetime.'

He let his gaze rove slowly over her slim form, then pinned her blue eyes with his own. 'For the record, my relationship with you is hardly paternal.'

His drawling tone caused her resentment to resurface. 'You're setting down rules, taking away my freedom of choice,' she retaliated, watching as he remained in the doorway.

'I've given you an option,' Luc corrected silkily.

'Sure, you have.' She speared him with an icy blue glare. 'With only one possible answer!'

He stepped into the lounge and shut the door. 'Did you imagine I'd have it any other way?'

Ana closed her eyes, then quickly opened them again. 'You've made it quite clear the child I carry is the main issue.'

She watched as he withdrew an envelope from the inside pocket of his jacket and extended it towards her. 'The legalities you requested.'

Stark legalese held an awful clarity she was loath to accept. Yet what other course did she have?

She lifted her head and met his steady gaze. There was a glimpse of something faintly dangerous in those dark depths she didn't care to define, and she returned her attention to the printed pages.

There were further clauses outlining conditions that covered every eventuality…and then some.

'You expect me to sign this?'

'A legal agreement was your idea.' Luc's tone was silk-smooth.

He was right. But that didn't make it any easier to attach her signature beneath his.

Luc took the document from her outstretched hand and tucked it into his jacket pocket. 'Do you want to eat out, or order in?'

Food? 'I thought you'd want to head back—' She paused, unable for the life of her to say *home*. 'To Sydney.'

'We,' Luc corrected, adding quietly, 'And you need to eat.'

'Such solicitousness is touching.'

'Don't be facetious.'

She spared him a long, thoughtful look, assessing the latent power, his innate sensual chemistry and its degree of sexual energy.

For the past nine days he'd filled her mind, invading it in a manner that was tortuous as she reflected on his long strong body, the feel of sinew and muscle, skin on skin, as his lovemaking transcended the physicality of mere sexual coupling.

It was there in his arms where she lost herself to any rational thought, and became a witching wanton eager to gift and receive each sensual delight.

For then she could qualify a one-sided love, content that it was *enough* not to have love returned in kind. She could even accept his heart remained locked in the memory of Emma, his first wife, hopeful that with time affection might become something deeper, more meaningful.

At no stage had she envisaged the existence or presence of a mistress.

And now there was to be a child...

She desperately wanted the marriage to survive. But there had to be trust, and honesty.

Was Luc's word, verbally and noted in legalese, sufficient?

After all, words were only an expression of intention, and easily disregarded or broken without honour.

'Are you done?'

The silkily voiced query held a slight edge which

snapped her back to the present, and her chin tilted in silent defiance. 'No.'

As long as she lived, she'd never be *done* with him. The trick was never to allow him that edge of knowledge.

His eyes narrowed slightly. 'How long will it take you to pack?'

She'd brought few clothes with her, bought less, and the little personal touches she'd added to the apartment would have no place in Luc's elegant Vaucluse mansion.

'I can be ready in fifteen minutes.' She could do *cool*. At least for now.

Without a further word she crossed into the bedroom, placed the empty bag onto a chair, and began the task of transferring her belongings.

Luc moved to the kitchen, opened the refrigerator and extracted bottled water, filled a glass and swallowed the chilled liquid.

Then he retrieved his cellphone, keyed in a series of digits and instructed his pilot to be on standby for the return flight.

There was, he decided grimly, no point in delaying the inevitable.

Don't look back, Ana bade silently as she walked at Luc's side to the car. He stowed her bag in the boot as she slid into the passenger seat, then within minutes he fired the engine and eased the car out from its parking bay.

Luc chose a restaurant at one of the upmarket hotels, and confirmation of their reservation indicated he'd phoned in ahead.

Her appetite seemed to have fled, and she picked at the starter, nibbled a few morsels from the artistically presented main, and chose fresh fruit in lieu of dessert.

'Not hungry?'

Ana spared him a level glance. 'No.' If he suggested she should eat more, she'd be hard pressed not to tip the contents of her plate into his lap.

Luc deferred to her preference for tea and ordered coffee for himself from the hovering waitress.

She watched as he spooned sugar into the dark brew, noting the shape of his hand, the skin texture and the tensile strength evident.

He had the touch, the skill, to drive her mindless with a tactile slide of his fingers, and she hated herself for the sudden increase in the beat of her heart.

Sexual chemistry. It had a power of its own. Damning, lethal.

It took considerable resolve to sip her tea with a semblance of calm, and she felt a sense of relief when he signalled the waitress for their bill.

Three quarters of an hour later they crossed the Tarmac and stepped aboard the luxurious Gulfstream jet, whose gently whining engines increased in pitch the instant the outer door closed.

Smooth, very smooth, Ana conceded minutes later as the jet wheeled its way out onto the runway, then cleared for take-off, gathered speed and rose like a silver bird into the sky.

The light was fading as dusk approached, and there was an opalescent glow as the sun slipped beneath the horizon in a brilliant flare of orange tinged with pink.

Darkness descended quickly, and all too soon there was nothing to see except an inky blackness and the occasional pinprick of lights as the jet followed the coastline south.

Ana made no attempt at conversation and simply leaned back against the headrest and closed her eyes, successfully shutting out the sight of the man seated at her side.

It didn't, however, shut out her chaotic thoughts.

A return to Sydney meant the re-emergence of the lifestyle she'd sought to briefly escape. There was her father, Rebekah, the florist shop.

Worst of all, there was Celine Moore. Her nemesis and her enemy.

Absenting herself for more than a week hadn't solved a thing. The problems remained. A hollow laugh rose and died in her throat. All that had been achieved was a metaphorical stay of execution.

Who would win? The wife or the mistress?

CHAPTER THREE

'GOOD evening, Ms Dimitriades.'

Ana returned the greeting and offered Petros a
faint smile as she slid into the rear passenger seat,
aware that Luc crossed behind the vehicle and
slipped in beside her.

Within minutes Petros eased the car forward,
cleared the private sector and joined the flow of traffic vacating the airport.

At this time of night they'd make good time to
Vaucluse, and she sank back against the soft leather
upholstery, intent on viewing the passing surround-
ings.

Bright lights, coloured flashing neon…the muted
noise of a big, cosmopolitan city.

To her it was *home*, where she'd been born and
raised, with an endearing sense of the familiar.

A blustery shower sprang up, splattering the wind-
screen with fine rain-spray and diminishing visibility.

It seemed to close in, heightening the close con-
fines of the car and her proximity to the man seated
at her side.

Silence stretched between them like a yawning
chasm, and she thought of a safe topic of conversation, only to discard it. Why pretend?

Vaucluse was a prestigious suburb with magnificent views over the inner harbour, and Ana's nerves tensed as the car turned in between the electronically controlled gates leading to Luc's architecturally designed home.

Stretching over two blocks of land, the elegant double-storeyed mansion possessed imposing lines, archways, and high-domed windows. It was set in well-kept grounds, the sculptured gardens maintained by Petros, who resided in rooms above the garages, and whose duties covered numerous chores supplemented by twice-weekly household help.

The car drew to a halt beneath the wide portico, and Ana emerged before Petros could move round to open the door, thereby incurring his faintly pained expression.

She stood as Luc disabled the security system and unlocked the panelled double doors. He swung them wide and she entered at his side.

Marble floor tiles in varying shades of cream bordered by dark forest-green covered the spacious foyer, and there were expensive works of art gracing the walls. Formal lounge and dining-room were positioned to the right, informal rooms and a spacious study lay to the left. The focal point was a wide, sweeping marble staircase leading to the upper floor which held no fewer than four bedrooms, each with *ensuite*, the master suite, and a private sitting-room.

'I'll serve refreshments,' Petros indicated as he moved into the foyer after securing the doors.

'Not for me.' Ana softened her refusal with a slight smile, and made for the stairs. She felt disinclined to extend the façade any longer than necessary.

Luc followed in her footsteps, and she turned to face him as they reached the landing.

'I'd prefer to have a room of my own.'

His expression didn't change. 'No.'

Resentment flared. 'What do you mean...*no*?'

'I would have thought my answer held sufficient clarity.'

'I don't want to sleep with you.'

'Perhaps not...tonight,' he amended silkily, and caught the flicker of pain in those deep blue eyes before it was successfully hidden.

'Not *any* night!'

'Brave words, Ana.'

He moved ahead of her with indolent ease, her bag in hand, and she watched in silence as he entered the master suite only to emerge seconds later empty-handed.

She wanted to rail against him, hating the power he possessed and her inability to retaliate in kind. She was caught in a web, tied to him by the child she'd conceived, and held there by family loyalty.

'*Go to hell*, Luc,' she evinced bitterly as he drew level.

He paused, and caught hold of her chin, tilting it so she had little option but to meet his steady gaze.

'Careful, *pedhaki mou*. I might be tempted to take you there.'

Her eyes widened at the silkily voiced threat, and her lips shook slightly as his hand slid to cup her cheek. 'I don't scare easily.'

The edge of his mouth quirked. 'One of your admirable qualities.' He released her and moved towards the head of the stairs.

He would, she knew, check with Petros for any messages, make the required calls, scan his electronic mail, and deal with the urgent stuff...all of which could take half an hour, or more.

It gave her time...to do what? Settle in? The thought was laughable.

Ana entered the master bedroom and came to a halt a few steps into the large room. Nothing had changed...had she really expected it to?

The king-size bed with its dark, richly patterned duvet and numerous pillows was a focal point. Furniture comprised matching sets of multi-layered chest of drawers in varying heights, and there were dual *ensuites*, dual walk-in wardrobes. A deep-cushioned sofa and a chaise longue completed a room that was designed for comfort and pleasure.

Sensual pleasure.

A feathery sensation scudded the length of her spine, and she cursed beneath her breath as memories of what she'd shared with Luc in this room rose damnably to the surface.

Vivid, sexually electrifying, and shameless.

Dear heaven. How could she slip beneath those covers and pretend everything was the same?

It didn't bear thinking about. Yet she had to face the situation.

But not tonight, she determined as she crossed to the upholstered stool at the foot of the bed, caught up her bag and retreated to another room, where she unpacked an oversized T-shirt, toiletries, then crossed to the adjoining *en suite*.

She should phone her father, then her sister to let them know she was home. Although if either opted to call, it would be to her cellphone, and there was time enough tomorrow to apprise them both of her return.

Now all she wanted to do was undress and slip into bed. Although there were too many thoughts chasing through her brain to promote an easy slide into sleep.

She was wrong. The events of the day, the flight, each took their toll, and combined with the effects of pregnancy ensured she was asleep within minutes of her head touching the pillow.

Ana woke slowly, drifting pleasantly towards consciousness, unaware for a few disoriented seconds of her whereabouts.

Then it all came flooding back...the flight, Sydney, *Luc*.

Her eyes widened as she recognised the master

suite, the large bed…and the familiar dark-haired male head resting on the pillow beside her own.

How could she be *here* when last night…?

'You were asleep.' Luc's voice was an indolent drawl, and her gaze became trapped in his for a few heart-stopping seconds, then he shifted, moving that powerful frame into a sitting position with fluid ease.

Ana closed her eyes, then opened them again. There was too much warm olive-toned flesh moulded into enviable shape by muscle and sinew.

The smattering of chest hair made her fingers itch to tangle there, and she longed to reach up and curl her hands round his nape and drag his mouth down to hers.

Except she did none of those things. Instead anger rose to simmer beneath the surface as she sought to inch away from him.

'You have no right—'

'Yes, I do.' He lifted a hand and brushed back a swathe of hair from her cheek.

She scrambled to the side of the bed, only to have him reach out and halt her flight.

'Let me go!'

'No.'

She lashed out at him, and struggled wildly as he pulled her onto his lap. Not a good position, she discovered. She was too close, much too close. And the dictates of her brain were at variance with the demand of her senses.

The thought of succumbing was more than she

could bear, and she stilled, aware that fighting him was a futile exercise.

'Don't.' The single negative held a beseeching anguish. 'Please.'

It was the heartfelt plea that got to him, and he caught her chin between thumb and forefinger, tilting it to examine her features.

Her eyes were deep enough to drown in, their emotions stark with a vulnerability that twisted his gut, and his gaze narrowed at the fast-beating pulse drumming at the base of her throat.

Her mouth shook a little, and he watched as she sought control. But it was the shimmering moisture in her eyes, and the single escaping tear running in a slow rivulet down one cheek that tore a husky imprecation from his lips.

With incredible gentleness he smoothed the moisture with his thumb, then he lowered his head and trailed his mouth over her cheek.

He let the palm of one hand slip down her arm and settle against the curve of her waist.

Their child grew there, a tiny embryo that would succour and gain strength. Its existence touched him as nothing else could.

'Come share my shower.'

'I don't think so.' He couldn't know just how much it cost her to refuse. Yet to slip back easily into the relationship they'd shared would indicate she condoned his use of emotional blackmail... something she hated him for. And Celine...dear heaven, she didn't even want to go *there*!

She slid from his grasp, aware it was only because he let her, and she gathered fresh underwear and retreated into the *en suite*.

Her stomach felt as if it didn't belong to her, and she pressed a hand to her navel in an attempt to soothe the disturbance.

Fifteen minutes later, showered and dressed in tailored trousers, singlet top and jacket, she felt measurably better, and she caught up her shoulder bag and ran lightly down the stairs to the kitchen where Petros was preparing eggs Benedict and the smell of freshly brewed coffee was ambrosia.

'Luc is in the dining-room. You will join him there.' He spared her a warm smile. 'I have made you tea.'

'But I prefer—'

'Tea. Caffeine is not recommended during pregnancy.'

Ana wrinkled her nose at him, feeling her spirits lighten a little. 'Bossy, aren't we?' Hunger assailed her, and she took a slice of toast from the stacked rack Petros had just added to the breakfast trolley, nibbled on it, then filched a fresh strawberry and popped it into her mouth.

She curled both hands over the trolley handle. 'Want me to take this through?'

'Really, Ms Dimitriades,' the man chastised with

an aloofness that brought forth a smile. 'Most definitely not.'

'Don't you think you could call me *Ana*?' she cajoled, then added teasingly, 'I'm almost young enough to be your daughter.'

He drew himself up to his full height. 'You are the wife of my employer. I could not begin to be so familiar.'

A laugh bubbled up in her throat and escaped as a mischievous chuckle. 'You call him *Luc*,' she reminded, and met his level glance.

'We have known each other a long time.'

'So how many years do I have to wait before you accord me the honour of using my Christian name?'

'Five years,' he responded solemnly, skilfully transferring grilled bacon onto a heated platter and placing it on the trolley together with the eggs. 'At least.'

'In that case, I get to wheel the trolley.'

His mouth parted in silent protest, then he pursed his lips as he caught her cheeky grin, watching as she took care of the chore and leaving him to tidy the kitchen.

The informal dining-room was at the back of the house, overlooking the pool, and caught the morning sun.

Ana reached it in seconds and swept through the open door. 'Breakfast…at your service.'

Luc was seated at the head of the table, the day's

newspaper spread out in front of him, a half-finished cup of coffee to one side.

His jacket hung over the back of his chair, on top of which lay his tie. A briefcase and laptop rested on the floor near by.

He looked up at the sound of her voice, cast the trolley a quizzical glance, then folded the newspaper.

'How did you manage that?'

'Feminine wiles and logical rationale.' She shifted platters onto the table, added fresh coffee, tea, and toast, then she drew out a chair and sat down.

She poured herself tea, added milk, then helped herself to eggs and toast.

Heaven, she decided after the first mouthful. No one but Petros made eggs Benedict this good.

'I imagine you'll call your father and Rebekah this morning?'

'Yes.' She took a sip of tea, and felt her stomach settle. 'Dad, as soon as I finish this.' She indicated the plate with her fork. 'Then I'll go into the shop.'

'Not to work.'

There was almost an edge of command apparent, and she paused in the process of transferring a portion of food to her mouth. 'Of course, to work.'

'There's no need for you to work.'

'Are we talking *today* specifically?'

'At all.' There was no mistaking the clarification.

'Now that I'm pregnant?' Her voice was quiet, too quiet.

'I don't see the necessity for you to be on your

feet all day, put in long hours, and become over-tired.'

She replaced her cutlery with care and pushed her plate aside. 'Instead, you'd prefer me to join the so-cial-luncheon set, shop a lot and rest each afternoon like a delicate swan?'

'You can shift your interest in the shop to that of silent partner, and have Rebekah employ an assis-tant.'

'No.'

'I'm not giving you an option.'

His voice was silk-smooth with an edge of anger she chose to ignore.

'Don't try to manipulate me, Luc.' Heat flared, turning her eyes into brilliant blue shards. 'I won't stand for it.'

'Finish your breakfast.'

'I've lost my appetite.' She stood to her feet and tossed the napkin onto the table. 'I have a few calls to make.'

He caught hold of her arm, halting her flight, and she had no illusions his grasp would tighten if she attempted to struggle.

'Tell Rebekah to employ your replacement.' Those who knew him well would have blanched at the silk-iness in his tone, recognised the predatory stillness apparent...and quailed. 'Or I will.' He waited a beat. 'Meanwhile, ensure your time at the shop is kept to a minimum.'

'Go to hell.'

His gaze chilled. 'Don't push me too far.'

She ignored the urge to respond as he released her arm. Instead she chose dignified silence, and walked out onto the terrace and descended the few steps to the garden.

There, she extracted her cellphone and called her father, confirmed her return and suggested lunch, only to have it postponed due to a business meeting until the following day.

He sounded distracted, anxious. Regretful?

Dammit, she wanted answers, or at least a reason *why* a man known for his loyalty and integrity had done something so out of character. And she needed to hear it from *him*.

But not today, she conceded as she retraced her steps.

CHAPTER FOUR

PETROS was clearing the table when she entered the dining-room.

'Luc has left for the city.'

'I'll need the keys to my car.'

The manservant continued loading the trolley with breakfast dishes. 'I don't think that's a good idea.'

Ana spared Petros a level glance. 'Luc is aware of my plans for the day.'

'Didn't agree with them, though, did he?'

'I have things to do, places to go.'

'The shop,' Petros concluded. 'Where you'll work all day.'

'I help run a business,' she reminded firmly.

'Luc will disapprove.'

She picked up her satchel, slung the strap over one shoulder and collected her car keys. 'I'll make sure he knows you told me so.'

'I'll drive you.'

'Thanks.' She was aware just how deep the man's loyalty went to his employer. 'But, no thanks.'

The shop was situated among a group of boutique shops in trendy Double Bay, and possessed a regular clientele.

Rebekah had a talent assembling flowers into an

art form, and went the extra mile to match blooms to both the recipient and the occasion. Ana took care of business...ordering, supplies, overseeing deliveries, liaising with the customers.

Wire, scissors, ribbon...and more than a little magic had earned Blooms and Bouquets a well-deserved reputation.

Ana entered the shop just after nine, and breathed in the scent filling the air, sharp and sweet, heady.

The slim blonde arranging blooms in a decorative basket glanced up at the sound of the electronic bell.

'Ana! It's so good to see you! When did you get back?'

'Last night.'

Ana found herself caught in an affectionate hug, from which she disentangled herself to meet Rebekah's keen appraisal.

'OK, what gives?'

'As in?'

'Your cryptic phone messages didn't come close to explaining the reason you flew the coop. And I don't buy Celine was the only reason,' Rebekah warned. 'So *tell* me.'

She could prevaricate, but what was the point? 'I'm pregnant.'

There was initial surprise, then her sister's mouth curved into a warm smile and her eyes lit up with pleasure, only to narrow slightly seconds later. 'So how come you're not dancing with joy?'

'It wasn't planned.'

Rebekah appeared sceptical. 'And that's a problem?'

'Not exactly.'

'But something's bothering you. Want to share?'

She was silent a few seconds too long, and Rebekah's voice gentled a little.

'Have you told Luc the extent of Celine's interference? Or just how vicious she's been?'

What difference would it make? 'No.'

'Don't you think you should?'

'I can handle Celine.'

'Darling,' Rebekah cautioned in rebuke. 'Given half a chance she'll eat you up and spit you out.'

Ana offered her sister a wry smile. 'Thanks for the vote of confidence.'

'I care about you.' She waited a beat. 'That's it? There's nothing else?'

Ana was torn between confiding their father's problems, and keeping silent. 'Blame it on raging hormones,' she dismissed with a negligible shrug, and even managed a rueful laugh.

'At a guess, my gorgeous brother-in-law would prefer his wife to remain at home?'

It was nothing less than the truth. 'Got it in one.'

'So that's why you came into work?'

A faint smile curved the edges of her mouth. 'You know me well.'

'As I have no wish to have Luc flay me alive,' Rebekah declared judiciously, 'from this day forward I take care of any heavy stuff. OK?'

'Maybe.'

'And you take an hour for lunch.'

'A concession I don't need.'

'You do the computer stuff.'

Ana assumed a pained look. 'Who said you get to be *boss*?'

Rebekah gave her a cheeky grin. 'I do.'

'Like I'll listen?'

'You could try.'

She deposited her bag, snagged a uniform cover-all and donned it, then crossed to examine the order book. 'OK, let's get to it.'

They worked together with the ease of long practice, and the deliveries went out on time, the Interflora orders were dealt with, and there was genuine pleasure in consulting with a prospective bride wanting something different for her bridal bouquet.

Ana was unpacking roses, glorious, long-stemmed, tight-budded blooms, when Rebekah handed her the cordless phone.

'The father of your child.'

Checking up on her. 'Luc,' she acknowledged, and heard his silky drawl in response.

'I thought we agreed you'd limit your hours at the shop.'

'I don't recall accepting your suggestion to do so.'

'Don't split hairs.'

'Is that what you think I'm doing?'

'Ana.' His voice held a warning threat she chose to ignore.

'Your concern is touching.'

'We'll continue this discussion later.'

'I can't wait.' She ended the call before he had a chance to utter a further word.

Not a good move, she reflected, given they were dining out that evening with friends. Correction…a few of Luc's colleagues and their partners. Wives, girlfriends, and mistress.

Ana had no doubt Celine Moore would make sure of the inclusion in a continuing effort to put the cat among the pigeons. The glamorous Celine was the queen of all felines…dangerous and deadly. While women recognised her power and were disturbed by it, men looked no further than stunning looks and her incredible sexuality.

Reneging on the evening was out of the question, and Ana felt the onset of nervous tension as the afternoon drew to a close.

'Go home,' Rebekah advised. 'I can manage things here until we close.'

'That bad, huh?'

'Nothing a leisurely shower and skilfully applied make-up won't fix.'

Ana rolled her eyes. 'Thanks.'

'You're welcome.' Rebekah offered a cheerful grin. 'Wear something gorgeous, and go knock Celine off her perch.'

'As if. She has claws of steel.'

'You have a few advantages. As well as Luc's ring on your finger, you're carrying his child.'

'The ring hasn't had any effect. What makes you think pregnancy will?'

Rebekah shot her a level look. 'We're talking *Luc*,' she reminded. 'Not someone like the rat I married and divorced in record time.'

Ana was all too aware of the impact an unsuccessful marriage had on her sister's life, the bitterness and rejection, the heartache. Three years had helped heal the wounds, but the emotional scars ran deep, leaving a wariness and distrust of men.

Support was a given, but she'd learnt to hold back on expressing verbal sympathy. Only a caring few knew Rebekah's hard exterior was merely a shell she wore to protect an inner vulnerability.

How would Rebekah react on hearing her brother-in-law had utilised emotional blackmail to bring Ana home?

'Go,' Rebekah bade. 'I'll do the markets.'

'That's unfair.' Sharing the pre-dawn run to buy fresh flowers at the markets each day was a given. 'I'm pregnant, not sick. Besides, you've had to do it while I was away.'

'I doubt Luc will hear of it.'

'Luc,' she assured, 'doesn't dictate my life.'

It wasn't something she wanted to give much thought to as she fought the late-afternoon traffic *en route* to his palatial home.

Petros greeted her as she entered the foyer. 'Luc will be delayed a half-hour, Ms Dimitriades.'

'Ana,' she corrected for the umpteenth time, aware

having Petros use her Christian name was a battle she'd probably never win.

The man's role was multi-faceted, at times his manner bore resemblance to military training. His age was indeterminable, but she pinned it between early-to-mid-fifties, and there was a sharpness about him that belied his household position.

General factotum, without doubt, but she was unable to shake the suspicion he also acted as bodyguard on occasion.

When she'd queried Luc, he merely relayed Petros had moved from his late father's employ to his own.

'It would be disrespectful for me to be so familiar with the boss's wife.'

Exasperation tinged her voice. 'Oh, put a sock in it.'

'Where precisely should I put the sock?'

She was strongly tempted to tell him. Instead, she chose silence, squared her shoulders and mounted the stairs with as much dignity as she could muster.

Selecting what to wear should have been simple, except there were too many choices. Classic black, or scarlet? Maybe the emerald sheath? One of the pastels with its floating chiffon panels?

Fifteen minutes later she threw her hands up in the air, tossed a black sheath with a lace overlay onto the bed, retrieved black stiletto-heeled pumps and caught up filmy black underwear *en route* to the *en suite* bathroom.

When she emerged Luc was in the process of discarding his clothes, and her heart faltered, then missed a beat as he shrugged out of his shirt.

Broad shoulders were accentuated by superb musculature and smooth-textured skin. A smattering of chest hair tapered down over his midriff and disappeared beneath his waistline.

She retained a vivid memory of what it was like to touch his warm flesh, to feel the flexing of muscle beneath her tactile exploration...with the pads of her fingers, her lips. The slide of her body on his, the faint hiss of his breath as he sought control. Her own barely audible groan as heat spiralled and encompassed every nerve-end until she became lost in shimmering sensation...sizzling, unprincipled, *raw*.

Slim-fitting black silk hipster briefs barely covered tight buttocks, and as he shifted she caught sight of the powerful bulge of his arousal.

Dear God, what was the matter with her that she stood here transfixed by the mere sight of him?

How *could* she be turned on, when she believed she had every reason to hate him?

With deliberate movements she sank down onto the edge of the bed and pulled on tights, smoothing them over each calf, then her thighs.

Unbidden, her gaze flicked towards him, and became trapped in his own.

For one heart-stopping minute everything remained still. There was only him, and the electric tension that fizzed between them like a broken live wire curling at random. Dangerous, deadly.

Then in seeming slow motion he stripped the silk briefs from his body, and walked with blatant unconcern into his *en suite*.

Seconds later the hiss of the shower acted as the catalyst that released her limbs from their trance-like state.

With shaky movements she caught up her dress, stepped into it, then slid home the zip.

Hair and make-up took longer than she anticipated.

Her fingers shook as she pinned up her hair into a fashionable knot, and she winced more than once when she jabbed her scalp. The application of eyeshadow and eyeliner required a skill that had suddenly gone haywire, and she had to start over twice before she achieved a desired result.

She was aware the moment Luc re-entered the bedroom, and she sensed his swift appraisal, felt the lick of heat sweep through her veins in damning recognition of his presence…and deliberately turned away to select minimum jewellery.

It didn't help that her senses were alert to the brush of silk against his body, the faint rustle of fine cotton as he added a shirt, or that her imagination ran riot at the thought of trousers by Armani being pulled up over powerful, hair-roughened thighs, followed by the almost silent snap of a waist fastener, the soft, sliding close of a zip.

Sensual warmth pooled deep within, radiating to a heavy ache that heightened her senses to quivering *need*.

Was he similarly affected? Somehow she doubted it.

And she was caught in a web of pride, anger and resentment that forbade her making the first move.

Was he game-playing? For a man with a high sex drive...

Her mind came to a screeching halt, and her body stilled. Had he seen Celine in her absence? The mere thought that he might have tore the breath from her body.

Dear heaven... *No*. The rebuttal was a silent scream. Fidelity. He'd given his assurance on that score, even put it in writing. Except they were only words. And Celine was a seductive temptress most men would find difficult to resist.

Men are from Mars, Women are from Venus. Wasn't that the catch-phrase of the new millennium? Concisely translated...women wanted love; men wanted sex.

'Problems?'

Her fingers fumbled with the clasp at her nape. 'I can manage.' Except attaching the fastener remained elusive, and she was supremely conscious of him as he crossed to her side, removed the gold chain from her nerveless fingers and smoothly tending to its closing.

Did he stand there a few seconds longer than necessary? Was the slight brush of his fingers against her nape deliberate, or merely accidental?

Get a grip! The silent chastisement held self-derision as she slid her feet into stiletto pumps and caught up an evening bag.

'Ready?'

Ana turned to face him and met the bland expression in those dark eyes. 'As ready as I'll ever be.'

Their hosts resided in a restored mansion right in the heart of Double Bay, where street parking was the only option and therefore made recognition of fellow guests' cars almost an impossibility.

Trendy cafés, narrow terrace houses converted into boutiques lent a cosmopolitan air where the wealthy lingered over lattes and watched the social élite mix and mingle.

The mesh shrieked both old and new money that reflected an eclectic style not generally seen anywhere else in the city.

Ten guests were assembled in the magnificent lounge, and Ana wasn't conscious of holding her breath until she released it in a tiny rush on discovering Celine was nowhere in sight.

She requested orange juice, and sipped it as she was drawn into conversation by a mutual acquaintance who seemed intent on lauding the expertise of the cosmetic surgeon currently in vogue.

Scintillating conversation, she accorded mentally, wondering at the priorities in some women's lives. Yet looking good was important if they wanted to keep a wealthy husband who provided the lifestyle they enjoyed, for there was always a younger version waiting in the wings, willing and eager to please.

Working out, enhancing the muscle-toned body, the regular manicures, pedicures, hair-styling, facials, body massage, the designer clothes, jewellery...all to gild what they perceived as a required image. As the years passed, the more desperate they became, and 'going abroad' was a well-touted excuse to have the latest 'nip and tuck' in America, Switzerland or France.

'What do you think, darling?'

'You'd never know,' Ana responded, dutifully endorsing the cosmetic surgeon's success.

'He's incredible. Frightfully expensive, of course. But then...'

'One must do what one has to do.'

'Absolutely.'

The guest moved on, and seconds later Luc curved an arm across the back of her waist.

'Don't you think you're taking togetherness a little too far?'

'No.'

'Forgive me. I forgot we're playing a game.'

'And that is?'

'Happily married,' she said without missing a beat.

His gaze narrowed. 'Careful, *kyria*. There's a limit to my patience.'

'As there is to mine.'

It was at that precise moment the hired help ushered in the last guest, and all heads turned as one at the sound of that husky feminine laugh.

Celine. The dark hair was beautifully coiffed, her

make-up spectacular; the woman could rival any international model. Add stunning looks, symmetrically perfect features, and she was a knock-out.

Partnering her was her handbag for the evening…a handsome man whose polished good looks and manner were almost too much for any mortal male.

A model? A gentleman escort who hired out his services?

Not nice, Ana alluded cynically, and mentally chastised herself for being uncharitable.

The air-kiss routine was a little too contrived to be genuine, Celine's gaze brittle, and there was a lack of warmth in her smile.

Like a pre-set guided missile she turned towards Luc and shot him a stunning glance that conveyed to everyone present just *who* she intended to target her attention.

Ana could almost *hear* the unspoken threat…and felt her stomach muscles clench in silent antipathy.

'The evening's entertainment has arrived,' she said quietly, and felt Luc's fingers tighten at the edge of her waist.

'Behave.'

'I wouldn't dream of doing anything else.' She hardly had time to take a breath, and Celine was before them, exuding an exotic blend of expensive perfume, and a gown that looked as if it had been sprayed on, so lovingly did it hug her slender curves.

'*Luc*, darling.'

The brush of her lips to his cheek was more than

a mere salutary greeting, and Ana gritted her teeth in vexation.

'Celine.' An acknowledgment that was polite to the extreme, and her smile a mere facsimile.

The seating at dinner was either badly mismanaged or created by adroit manipulation on Celine's part.

One could almost be amused by it, Ana decided with resignation as she sank into a chair opposite Celine's partner.

There were numerous ways she'd choose to spend an evening, but observing her husband's ex-mistress eating him alive across the table wasn't one of them.

It was a great shame she couldn't indulge in a glass of wine to dull the edges, and food didn't quite do it for her. In fact, given the way her stomach was behaving, she had to wonder whether food of any kind was advisable.

'Dieting, darling?'

Implication was the mother of invention. 'Coping with a migraine.' Not entirely untrue, for a few hours in Celine's company was guaranteed to provide Ana with a headache.

Celine effected a faint moue, and directed at Luc a warm seductive smile.

Ana speared a prawn with unnecessary vigour, and attempted to do justice to the delectable starter.

The main dish followed, and she took minuscule servings, which she subsequently picked at, only to discard her cutlery after a few morsels.

Conversation flowed, as did the wine, and she had to wonder if she was the only person who noticed Celine's increasingly seductive behaviour.

There was a moment where Celine cast Luc a particularly blatant smile and deliberately moistened her lips, causing Ana to gnash her teeth.

She was sorely tempted to pick up her glass and throw iced water in Celine's face. If nothing else, it might cool her down.

Except such an action would only cause an unforgivable scene.

It was during dessert that she felt something touch her leg.

Accidental, or contrived to draw Ana's attention to the fact Celine was grazing a sheer Lycra-clad toe against Luc's leg beneath the table...or worse?

Enough, Ana decided, was *enough*.

'Lost your shoe, Celine?'

Ana had to give her credit...the woman was a superb actress.

'No. What makes you think that?'

Give it up, Ana decided. Here, *now*, was not the time or the place for a showdown. Instead, she curled the fingers of her left hand into a fist beneath her napkin, and barely restrained herself when she felt Luc's hand close over her own.

To what purpose? Silent commiseration, or an attempt to soothe her suspicions?

With a surreptitious movement she shifted her fist

to his thigh, and dug her nails into solid muscle...hard.

To give him credit, he gave no indication there was a silent battle of wills being played out of sight. Instead he merely uncurled her fingers and lifted them to his lips in a gesture that brought a slight stain of pink colour to her cheeks.

Only Ana glimpsed steel beneath the projected warmth evident in that dark gaze...and something else she didn't care to define. Anger, annoyance?

She told herself she didn't care.

'One trusts you enjoyed your sojourn on the Coast?'

Why did she have the impression no conversation with Celine was safe? The words were politely couched, the tone innocuous. Except she knew all too well how Celine operated, and *innocence* wasn't on her agenda.

'It proved to be a pleasant break.'

A perfectly shaped eyebrow rose fractionally. 'Alone?'

Oh, my, it was like tiptoeing through a minefield!

'You find that surprising?'

'Luc appeared a little distracted by your absence.'

Ana swept his strong features with amusing warmth, lingered over-long on his generously curved mouth and endeavoured to control the shivery sensation feathering down her spine. 'How nice to be missed.'

He still retained hold of her hand, and she attempted to pull it free without success.

This close she was aware of the subtle and expensive brand of his cologne mingling with the fabric of his clothes, the warmth of his skin. Apparent was a sexual energy, giving hint to a raw primitiveness that was exciting and vaguely frightening.

It brought forth vivid memories of their lovemaking…the wildness, the hunger, and the tenderness.

She missed the closeness, his touch, the times she lay in his arms living the moment when it was almost possible to believe he cared.

Except there was always a degree of control, something he never quite lost, and she wondered what it would take to have him become totally mindless.

Did he know how she felt? Dear heaven, how could he not?

'Shall we adjourn to the lounge for coffee?'

Ana opted for tea, and sipped the mild brew slowly as she stood at Luc's side.

Celine seemed intent on bewitching her companion for the evening…an action surely designed to make Luc aware what he was missing.

Were fellow guests observing Celine's charade? Or was she being overly sensitive?

'Finished?'

She glanced at Luc as he removed the cup and saucer from her hand. 'Thank you.'

'Shall we leave?'

A faint smile curved the edges of her mouth. 'I thought you'd never ask.'

Playing *polite* for the past few hours had taxed her acting skills. *Get used to it,* a tiny voice taunted.

His gaze narrowed. 'Tired?'

'If I say *yes*, will it invite a lecture?'

'Without doubt.'

'Then *no*, I'm not tired.'

'You're pale,' he observed.

'And your beard-shadow is beginning to show.'

A humorous gleam showed momentarily in those dark eyes, then it was gone, and she tried not to stiffen as he placed an arm across the back of her waist.

It took a while to reach the car, for there were the shared reminders of upcoming events, two extended invitations to consider, and the inevitable delay before the last 'goodnight' was exchanged.

The vehicle purred through the quiet street, and Ana leant her head back against the cushioned rest and closed her eyes.

She didn't feel like rehashing the evening, or querying any one of Celine's actions.

Soft music floated out from the speakers, and she felt the breath sigh from her body as tense muscles began to relax.

There was a part of her that wanted to weep for what she couldn't have; another part needing to scream at Celine for deliberately setting out to take what little she did have.

Instead, she did neither, and when the car drew to a halt in the garage she released the seat belt, slid to her feet, and as soon as Luc deactivated the security system, she entered the house and made her way upstairs without uttering so much as a word.

He didn't follow, and she undressed, removed her make-up, then unpinned her hair and slid into bed.

It was a while before Luc entered the bedroom, and he unhooked his jacket, released his tie, toed off his shoes, then stripped down to silk briefs before crossing to stand looking down at the woman who was his wife.

Vulnerable in sleep, she appeared almost fragile. Her skin had a translucent quality, and he wanted to brush the pads of his fingers over its softness, and push back the swathe of hair that rested against her cheek.

Slender shoulders, feminine, muscle-toned arms, and delicate hands. Capable hands, which were quick and deft, slim fingers with nicely shaped polished nails.

He winced at the memory of how they'd dug into his flesh only hours before, and the edge of his mouth quirked in humour at the reason why.

There was the knowledge he could slide in beneath the covers and reach for her, aware that in sleep she wouldn't resist. The touch of his lips to the sensitive hollow at the edge of her throat, the fleeting trail of his fingers to the swell of her breast...the unerring path to the moist crevice at the apex of her thighs.

He could cajole with expertise, utilise unfair persuasion, and she would be his.

Except he wanted her awake and aware, to come to him with warmth and need in her heart. More, much more than that, he wanted all that she could gift him...with her generous willingness of spirit, from the depths of her soul.

And that, he accepted, wasn't going to happen any time soon.

CHAPTER FIVE

ANA had nominated a restaurant not far from Blooms and Bouquets for lunch with her father.

Although the occasion proved something of an anticlimax, for he arrived late, greeted her affectionately, then he apologetically declared he couldn't stay long.

Of average height, he'd always had a presence. It was in the way he held himself, the easy way he moved. Yet today he seemed... Diminished, she perceived a trifle sadly.

They ordered from the menu, and sipped chilled water as they waited for their food.

'Are you OK?'

Was it something in her tone that caused the pain reflected in his eyes?

'Luc told you.'

To pretend ignorance was a useless exercise, and she hated the guilt that momentarily haunted his features.

'Did you think he wouldn't?'

He had the grace to look embarrassed.

What would his reaction be if she confided Luc had used the knowledge as leverage to effect a reconciliation?

A waiter served their order, and they both ate, mindful of the need not to linger.

'I only have one question,' Ana began without pre-amble. *'Why?'*

'There was a woman…' Her father paused, then continued with obvious reluctance. 'By the time I discovered she was playing at least three men against each other, I'd run up a fortune on credit.'

The most immediate question came to mind. 'What will you do now?'

'Sell the apartment, and try to rebuild my reputa-tion. Overseas,' he elaborated. 'I have connections in New York.'

Maybe it would be a good move, and she told him so.

'Did you enjoy the Coast?'

'It's good to be back.' A fabrication, yet the stark truth wasn't something she was prepared to confide. Although there was something she could share, and did. 'How do you feel about becoming a grandfa-ther?'

His smile reflected pleasing warmth, and he cov-ered her hand with his own. 'Are we talking a *fait accompli*?'

It was after two when Ana returned to the shop, and the remainder of the afternoon passed quickly as she brought computer records up to date, dealt with accounting entries, and handled the phone.

Traffic was heavy, and it took a while to reach Vaucluse. The thought of a shower, changing into casual clothes, and a long, cool drink…in that order, was uppermost in her mind as she garaged the car.

A light meal, maybe she'd view a video, then she'd catch an early night.

Petros emerged into the foyer as she entered it, and she offered him a stunning smile. 'Hi, how was your day?'

'The usual, Ms Dimitriades. And yours?'

'The same.' Her response held a musing solemnity that wasn't lost on the manservant.

'Luc asked that I inform you he'll be late. A business dinner, I understand.'

'So it's just me, and the kitchen cat. A salad will be fine.'

His lips thinned in visible disapproval. 'I have prepared something more substantial than a salad. If you'll kindly tell me where and at what time you'd like to eat, I will be on hand to serve the meal.'

'And the kitchen cat?' It was a query she couldn't resist, and brought forth the glimmer of a smile.

'Sulked the entire time you were absent.' As did the master of the house, although one didn't use *sulk* and *Luc Dimitriades* in the same sentence. A heightened temperament was more appropriate.

'Then I should make amends.'

One would imagine if Luc owned a four-legged feline, it would be an exotic breed. Except Oliver had turned up at their back door a month ago, hungry, wet, and looking pitifully pathetic. Towelled dry, given a saucer of milk, he declared the house his new abode. And stayed. Supposedly consigned to the kitchen and laundry, he enjoyed the run of the house from morning until night.

'An excellent suggestion.'

Ana found Oliver curled in his laundry basket, and he eyed her carefully as if weighing up whether to greet her or not. She had, after all, not been around for a while. Except there was something in the tone of her voice, a caring gentleness to her touch that won him over, and he allowed instinct to rule by rolling onto his back.

Unconditional affection, Ana reflected as she stroked Oliver's arched throat, then his exposed belly.

If only it were as uncomplicated with the human species, she mused as she ascended the stairs to the upper floor.

After a leisurely shower she donned jeans, a blouse with its edges tied in a careless knot at her midriff, gathered the length of her hair into a careless knot, then she retraced her steps to the kitchen, where Petros was in the process of arranging a succulent stir-fry on a bed of steaming rice.

Ana caught up a fork and dipped it into the rice, directed Petros a cheeky grin at his mock-severity, and collected a plate. 'I'll go eat on the terrace.'

The air held the balmy warmth of early summer, and she had a yen to feel the slight breeze against her face, breathe in the faint scents of growing blooms, and gain some tranquillity.

'It's my job to serve you.'

She spared him a level glance and began spooning rice and stir-fry onto her plate. 'We've had this argument before.'

'I'm sure we'll have it again.' Petros released a long-suffering sigh. 'Luc would—'

'Luc isn't here,' she reminded solemnly. 'So do me a favour and lighten up.'

He appeared to tussle with his conscience. 'Very well.'

It was a beautiful evening, and the view from the terrace out over the inner harbour spectacular. Everything appeared so still, the water glassy-smooth with small craft moored close in to the rock-faced cliffs.

Above, the sky was pale with an opalescent glow that appeared as the sun sank lower towards the horizon. Soon streaks of colour in varied shades of rose-pink would appear, brightening to orange in a final flare before the dusk preceded night.

It was easy to let her mind wander back to the first time she came into this house. The pleasure in loving the man who'd brought her here, and the promise of what could and would be, in spite of the knowledge a part of his heart would always belong to Emma, the young girl he'd married and lost much too soon.

In the eleven years between his first and second marriage there had been women. A man of Luc's wealth and calibre was an inevitable magnet for female attention. She could accept that.

She could even handle the relatively harmless flirtatious games played out by the social set.

A mistress, however, was something she refused to condone.

Celine would have Ana believe the affair was alive and well. But was it? Luc swore *no*. So who did she believe?

'If you've finished, I'll take your plate.'

She turned at the sound of Petros's voice and offered him a winsome smile. 'Thanks. It was delicious.'

'Would you like some dessert? Fresh fruit?'

She shook her head.

'Some tea, perhaps?'

'I'll come in and get it.'

'Stay there.' He looked out over the gardens. 'It really is very pleasant at this time of evening.'

The edges of her mouth tilted. 'Conversation, Petros?' Her eyes assumed a slightly wicked gleam. 'You so rarely indulge.'

'I'll fetch your tea.'

Ana moved from the table and curled onto a nearby chaise longue. Seconds later there was a soft plop as a furry bundle landed beside her on the cushion and Oliver began systematically digging in his front paws, circled twice, then settled into a ball close to her thigh.

She lifted a hand and stroked the cat's head, then fondled his ears, and was rewarded with a quiet throaty purr.

'Well,' Petros exclaimed softly as he carefully placed a cup and saucer on the side-table. 'It appears he's decided to attach himself to you.'

Oliver lifted his head, offered Petros an unblinking feline stare, then rested his chin on his paws.

'I'll go fetch you a sweater.'

Ana sipped the tea, and when darkness fell she donned the sweater Petros brought, taking care not to disturb Oliver.

Electric street-lights were visible in the distance, and seemed to merge with stars in an inky sky. 'Would you like more tea?'

She turned towards Petros, whose silent tread she'd failed to detect. 'No, thanks.'

It was there Luc found her, asleep, her head resting against the cushioned rest.

She wasn't to know Petros had remained indoors keeping her in plain sight until Luc returned home. Or that both men exchanged brief words before the manservant crossed to the foyer and took the internal stairs to his flat.

Luc stood in front of the chaise longue, looking at her features in repose, then he hunkered down and gently tucked a stray tendril of hair behind her ear.

She stirred, and he cupped a palm over her shoulder and ran it lightly down to rest at her elbow, watching as her eyelashes fluttered, then swept slowly upward.

'What are you doing out here, *pedhi mou*? Stargazing?'

Ana reached out a hand and found an empty space where the cat had slept. 'Oliver?'

'Petros has settled him into his basket for the night.' He rose to his full height in one fluid movement, then he leant forward and lifted her into his arms.

She didn't feel inclined to struggle. 'I can walk.'

His mouth brushed her temple. 'Indulge me.' He carried her easily, dousing lights, setting the security alarm as he moved through the house, then he ascended the stairs and traversed the gallery to their bedroom.

'I don't think—'

His lips touched hers, savouring with a slow provocative sweep of his tongue. And left her wanting more.

He shouldered the door shut and advanced towards the bed. 'Is it so important that you think?'

She thought sadly of hopes and dreams, of what was, and what could be. Mostly, she thought of *now*.

'Yes.'

He slowly lowered her to her feet, and let his hands slip down to cup her bottom. Then his head descended, and his lips caressed hers with a gentleness that made her want to weep.

'I don't want to do this.'

It was an ache-filled whisper that curled around his heart and tugged a little.

'Then tell me to stop.'

Dear God…she hungered for his touch.

The slow, tantalising sweep of his tongue caused heat to lick through her veins, and her body swayed into his, as if driven there by a force stronger than she.

His mouth parted, moving hers to open to accept his probing exploration, and she whimpered in part need, part protest as he deepened the kiss.

He spread one hand over her buttocks and slid the other up her spine to hold fast her nape, and wrought havoc with her senses.

It wasn't enough, not nearly enough.

She needed to feel her skin against his, without the barrier of clothes, and her fingers tore at the buttons on his shirt, loosening them, then she dragged the cotton free from his trousers.

A low, guttural sound emerged from her throat as he pulled off her sweater, and followed it with her blouse, then her bra.

A hand shaped her breast, his thumb on one roseate peak, caressing until heat pooled at the juncture of her thighs, flaring in a radiating spiral that almost drove her mad.

Buttons, fasteners, each were undone in haste and fell to the carpet, quickly followed by silk, until there was nothing between them.

Ana cried out, and the sound became lost against the invasion of his mouth as he tumbled her carefully down onto the bed.

Then his body rose over hers, large, powerful, and fully aroused. His eyes were dark with passion, hard muscle and sinew corded as he supported his weight above hers.

There was leashed control apparent as he brought his mouth down to her breast, and suckled there, taking her almost to the edge of pain before trailing a path to her navel, pressing a tracery of light kisses over her stomach as he moved low.

She should cry out for him to halt this madness before it went any further. But she was powerless to utter so much as a word.

She needed his possession, craved it. To deny him was to deny herself, and she damned her sybaritic soul as he tipped her over the edge, then held her as she fell.

He entered her slowly, inch by exquisite inch until she thought she'd go mad. He was in control, his hands cupping each hip, holding her there as he set an unhurried rhythm that made her want to weep.

When she would have quickened and deepened the pace he brought his mouth down over hers in a kiss that alternately cajoled, caressed, *soothed*.

His release when it came completed her, and his shuddering body brought feminine satisfaction for as long as it took for her emotions to settle.

He lay on his side, facing her, with one arm tucking her body in close to his.

He pressed a kiss to the edge of her shoulder. '*Pedhi mou*, I adored your reluctance.'

'I hate you.'

'Uh-huh.' His lips reached her elbow, then trailed to the inside of her wrist.

'Celine—'

'Has no part in what we share together,' he assured, and felt the rapid acceleration of her pulse.

'That isn't how she sees it.'

His lips were as light as the brush from a butterfly's wing as he retraced a path and settled in the sensitive curve of her neck.

'You want to talk of another woman, when the only woman who interests me is *you?*'

Oh, God. He had the touch to drive her wild. 'They're only words.'

'What would you have me say?'

I love you. The silent, beseeching cry came from her heart. And it broke a little with the knowledge they were words he would never declare.

He reached down and drew the bedcovers over them both, then caught hold of her chin and tilted it so she had no choice but to look at him.

'You are mine, *kyria*. You carry my child. It is enough.'

He was wrong. It wasn't nearly enough.

'You want to continue this discussion?'

It took every effort to force her voice to sound calm. 'Why?' She swallowed the betraying lump in her throat. 'There is nothing to discuss.'

CHAPTER SIX

'YOU intend going in to the shop?'

She met his gaze across the breakfast table, then deliberately sipped her tea. 'Yes.'

'Deliberate defiance, Ana?'

She took a deep breath, then slowly released it.

'Rebekah has consigned me to taking orders, managing the computer records, and handling the phone. If necessary, we'll employ someone to help out. Satisfied?'

'Not entirely.'

'Tough.'

Something moved in the depths of his eyes. 'You're playing a dangerous game, *agape mou*.'

My lover. Did he imagine all it took was one night in his arms? 'Nothing has changed, Luc.'

'You think not?'

The insistent burr of her cellphone precluded the necessity to answer, and she read the text message, then gathered up her satchel. 'I have to go.'

He slid a hand through a swathe of her hair and held it firm as his mouth closed over hers in a brief evocative kiss that stirred her senses and left her wanting more.

Then she was free.

'Enjoy your day.'

She didn't want to think about the musing gleam in those dark eyes, nor the faintly mocking tone in his voice.

Nevertheless, both haunted her as she traversed the main thoroughfare leading towards Double Bay.

If Luc imagined *sex* resolved everything, then he was mistaken, she determined as she halted behind a stream of traffic waiting for the lights to change.

In the cool light of day there were several recriminations. Mostly against herself. For succumbing to Luc's seduction, and displaying only a token resistance to shared intimacy.

Warmth flooded her veins at the mere thought of the night, and her stomach did a slow somersault as she recalled her response.

The sound of a car horn heralded a return to the present, and it was almost eight when she entered the shop.

It proved to be a busy day, with numerous phone calls with delivery orders, which necessitated the need to order more stock to fill them.

'Go take a lunch break,' Rebekah urged. 'Sit outside in the fresh air at one of the sidewalk cafés. You can bring me back a sandwich, pastrami on rye with salad, mayo, and hold the mustard.'

It was a lovely day, a slight breeze teased the leaves in the tree-lined street, and warm sunshine filtered down from an almost cloudless blue sky.

Double Bay had a style all its own with élite boutiques, numerous cafés, and close to the sea there was a hint of it in the air, a freshness that meshed with mild early-summer temperatures.

She felt the need for exercise, and crossed the street to the next block, then chose a café where there were a few empty tables beneath sun umbrellas.

A waiter materialised from inside the café, took her order, and delivered it in record time. She viewed the tastefully presented chicken and salad sandwich with anticipation.

So far she had very few pregnancy symptoms except a faint queasiness first thing in the morning. But her appetite had changed, and it amused her the foetal infant's demands ran to six small meals a day instead of the normal three. If she failed to pander to its whims, the result was nauseousness. Definitely a babe with a mind of its own!

'Ana.'

Oh, lord, please, *no*, not Celine. But it was she, looking the glamour queen in impeccably styled clothes, and perfectly applied cosmetics.

'You don't mind sharing, do you?'

Now that was a dubious statement, if ever there was one. Did she mean to convey a *double entendre*? 'The table, Celine?'

'Of course, darling. I only want coffee.' She slid into a chair. 'And we need to talk.'

'We do?' She was strongly tempted to stand to her feet and leave. Except fascination kept her seated. 'Regarding?'

'Why, *Luc*, of course.'

Of course. Who else? Ana made a point of checking her watch. 'I'm due back at the shop in a few minutes.'

'Luc and I were discussing the situation yesterday.'

'Really?' She glimpsed the triumphant gleam apparent in the other woman's gaze, and slanted one eyebrow. 'A deliberate *oops* moment, Celine?'

'Luc and I go back a long way.'

She'd had enough. '*Back* is the operative word. As in *past*.' She stood to her feet and gathered up the bill. 'Do yourself a favour. Get over it, and move on.'

'Perhaps you should ask yourself why Luc chooses not to terminate the affair.'

She felt sickened by it all, the innuendo fed by her own self-doubt. Worse, the steady barbs of verbal poison Celine had delighted in aiming at every opportunity.

'Accept you've become obsessively compulsive over a man who doesn't want you.' Strong words, but she was way past abiding by the niceties of good manners. 'The *affair* finished before your marriage, and my own. As Luc tells it, your time together was brief, and it was he who ended the relationship.'

She felt slightly light-headed, almost faint. A rush of blood to the head? she queried silently in an attempt at wacky humour. 'I'm not into human *ownership*, Celine,' she managed calmly. 'If Luc wants to discard me and lose his marriage, he's perfectly free to do so.'

On that note she entered the café, collected Rebekah's sandwich to-go, paid the bill, then she left without so much as a glance in Celine's direction.

'You look…frazzled,' Rebekah commented when Ana entered the shop.

'Put it down to an unwelcome lunch guest.'

'Celine?'

'Ah.' She offered a sweet smile as she took a seat in front of the computer. 'You didn't even need three guesses to get it right.'

'She called into the shop, intent on cornering you. That woman is a pest.'

'You're not wrong.'

'What are you going to do about her?'

'You mean, apart from getting mad?' She downloaded the afternoon's batch of orders and printed them out. 'I'm handling it.'

'Maybe you should have Luc handle it.'

'Go running to him with a sob story that's as pitiful as it's pathetic? And admit I can't deal with it?' She punched in a code, and checked data on the screen. 'No. It's my problem, my call.'

Mid-afternoon Ana logged in an order for a delivery of flowers Friday afternoon together with an additional arrangement fee. It was a service Blooms and Bouquets offered, and had proven popular with numerous social hostesses when giving a private dinner party in their home.

Floral arrangement was an art form, and a professional could assemble an artistic display in a fraction of the time it would take the inexperienced.

However her heart seemed to miss a beat and falter when she wrote down the client's name, address and contact number.

Celine.

There had been no recognition, no personal greeting. Just the requisite facts.

The obvious question had to be *why* Celine had chosen Blooms and Bouquets when there were any number of florists with whom she could have placed the order.

The woman's motive had to be suspect. Mischief and mayhem? Without doubt, Ana concluded with a grimace.

'What's up?'

Ana gathered her wits together, and relayed the order.

'I'll take care of it,' Rebekah said at once.

'No. I will.' Celine obviously had no intention of giving up. 'This is another battle in an ongoing war,' she determined grimly.

'Luc won't approve.'

'He doesn't need to know.'

'He will,' Rebekah warned. 'Celine will make sure of it.'

'Her order makes it business,' she qualified.

'It's personal,' Rebekah argued. 'And we both know it.'

'So? What's the worst she can do?'

Celine's apartment was in an exclusive Rose Bay residential tower.

Obviously the divorce settlement had been favourable, Ana deduced as she entered a sumptuous suite whose visible decorative theme featured leopard print cushions scattered on off-white deep-cushioned sofas and single chairs, with stunning framed prints of prowling leopards in various poses adorning the walls.

Ana could almost hear their collective jungle snarl, and silently attributed Celine's choice as being strikingly pertinent to the woman's personality.

Neutral tones featured as a background, and she mentally selected the brilliant orange flash of strelitzia as the focal colour with a native mix in pale green and gold.

Celine's greeting lacked civility, but then she hadn't expected anything less. Today wasn't about floral arrangements. It was another step towards a war between two women who each wanted the same man.

However, she could at least get on with the pretence, and she went straight into professional mode. 'Shall we get started? It would help if you'll tell me the look you want to achieve.'

Maximum effect for less than minimum price, and heavily discounted at that, Ana perceived some time later as Celine threw every suggestion out the window.

'Work with me, Ana.' The haughty command held arrogance.

It was time for a reality check. 'What you want is unachievable for the price you're prepared to pay.'

'Your profit margin has to be outrageous.'

She wanted to turn on her heel and walk out. Almost did, except they were still on a business footing, albeit that it was shaky ground.

'Rebekah and I pride ourselves on the quality of the blooms we supply, and our fee is standard.'

She closed the display folder and slid it into her briefcase. 'I suggest you consult someone else.'

Celine's expression hardened. 'I really can't be bothered wasting any further time on this. Itemise your quote, and I'll sign it.'

Business was *business*. Ana set everything down in meticulous detail, checked it, acquired Celine's signature, and gave her the customer copy.

Celine flicked the paper with a lacquered nail. 'For this amount, I'll expect perfection.'

'I doubt you'll have any reason to complain.' But you'll do your best to find something to denigrate Blooms and Bouquets, and take great pleasure in doing so.

Ana should have taken notice of her initial instinct and refused the job. So why hadn't she? Sheer stubborn-mindedness in not allowing Celine to triumph in any way.

'I hope you don't think you've won.'

Ah, the real purpose for her presence here. 'I wasn't aware we were in competition.'

'Don't play me for a fool.'

'I would never do that.'

'Just think, darling.' Celine's false smile took on a spiteful quality. 'I had Luc before you. Remember that, and wonder how you could possibly be an adequate substitute.'

'Yet you married someone else.' She couldn't help herself. 'One can only imagine it was because Luc didn't ask you?'

'Bitch.'

'Go get a life, Celine. And stay out of mine.'

'Not a chance. There isn't a thing you could say or do that would influence me.'

'I'm carrying Luc's child.'

Celine arched a brow in supercilious condemnation. 'And that's supposed to send me into retreat mode?'

'Forgive me, I forgot you don't possess any scruples...moral, or otherwise.'

'Got it in one, darling.' Celine examined her perfectly manicured nails, then speared Ana with a killing glance. 'Don't for a minute think you have an advantage in spawning a Dimitriades heir.' Her laugh portrayed the antithesis of humour as she raked Ana's slender form. 'Pregnancy isn't an attractive look. Who do you think Luc will turn to when you resemble a waddling whale?'

'You've mixed metaphors,' Ana managed calmly.

Quite a feat when *calm* didn't come close to the anger burning inside. 'And some men are blown away by a woman's conception.'

'Poor Ana.' Condescension positively dripped off her tongue. 'You're delusional if you imagine Luc is one of them.'

It was time to leave before she said or did something regrettable.

'Good afternoon, Celine.' Ana moved into the foyer and let herself out the door. Her steps were measured as she crossed to the lift, and it was only when she cleared the building that she allowed herself to vent some of her pent-up anger.

There were two messages on her voice-mail. Luc, and Rebekah. She used speed-dial to connect with her sister.

'Problems?'

'Just checking to see if you weathered the Celine appointment OK.'

'It could have been worse. I'll be at the shop in fifteen minutes.'

She reached Luc on his private line, and attempted to control her spiralling emotions as he picked up.

'Dimitriades.'

'You left a message to call.'

'So I did.' His voice was a faintly inflected drawl, and she envisaged him leaning back in his chair.

'I'm about to get into the car and drive,' Ana warned.

'So keep it brief?'

She could sense the wry humour in his voice, and retaliated without thought. 'Yes.'

'Jace is flying in from the States on Sunday. Ask Rebekah to join us Monday evening for dinner.'

The Dimitriades men were from the same mould…tall, dark, ruggedly attractive, and dynamite with women. Jace Dimitriades was no exception.

'Playing matchmaker, Luc?'

'The suggestion came from Jace,' Luc responded, indolently amused, and Ana gnashed her teeth, all too aware of the tension that existed between her sister and Luc's cousin.

'Don't plan on Rebekah accepting.'

'*No,*' Rebekah refused emphatically less than twenty minutes later. 'Not in this lifetime.'

'OK.'

'Just—*OK*? You're not going to cajole, persuade, twist my arm?'

'No.'

'Jace is—'

Ana offered a cynical smile. 'Another Luc?'

'Quite capable of issuing an invitation himself,' Rebekah completed.

'Which you'll have the greatest pleasure in refusing?'

'Yes.'

It was as well the phone rang, and Rebekah took the call while Ana crossed to the computer.

'Dad,' Rebekah informed as she replaced the handset. 'He wants us to join him for dinner…

tonight. Says it's very important.' She cast Ana a pensive glance. 'Do you have any idea what it's about?'

Oh, lord. The whole truth wouldn't sit well. Perhaps she could get by with imparting only some of it?

'He mentioned having contacts in New York when we had lunch yesterday.'

Rebekah's gaze sharpened. 'You think he might consider taking a position there?'

'I guess it's possible.' Why did she feel as if she was digging a proverbial hole with every word she spoke?

'Presumably he'll tell us about it tonight.'

Which meant she should ring Luc and tell him she wouldn't be home for dinner.

He was in a meeting, and she sent him a text message, then didn't bother checking her cellphone until she arrived home.

'Luc will be delayed until six-thirty,' Petros informed when she walked through the door.

By which time she'd be on her way into the city to meet her father and Rebekah…if she was lucky. 'Thanks.'

She headed for the stairs, and on reaching the bedroom she stripped, took the quickest shower on record, then dressed with care in an elegantly tailored ultra-violet trousersuit.

Ana was putting the finishing touches to her makeup when Luc entered the room. He'd loosened his tie, undone the top few buttons on his shirt, and he held his jacket hooked over one shoulder.

He looked the powerful magnate, a sophisticate whose forceful image projected an dramatic mesh of elemental ruthlessness and latent sensuality.

His eyes were dark, almost still, and her heart jolted a little in reaction. There was a part of her that wanted to close the space between them, touch light fingers to his cheek, then pull his head down to hers in a kiss that invited as much as it promised.

She wanted to smile, and offer 'Tough day?', then share her own in musing commiseration.

Except she did none of those things. Instead, she dropped a lipstick into her evening bag and caught up her keys.

'You got my text message?'

Luc tossed his jacket down onto the bed, and pulled his tie free. 'Yes.' He began releasing the buttons on his shirt, then pulled it free from his trousers. 'Petros will drive you. Ring me when you're through, and I'll come collect you.'

'Don't be ridiculous. I'll drive myself.'

'No,' he said evenly. 'You won't.'

Anger rose with simmering heat. 'The hell—'

His eyes seared hers, dark and infinitely dangerous. 'We can do this the hard way,' he relayed silkily. 'The result will be the same.'

'Aren't you overreacting just a touch?'

'It's not open to negotiation.' He toed off his shoes, then released the zip on his trousers. 'You *want* to circle the city streets trying to find a parking space? Walk alone in the dark to the restaurant venue?' His voice held a chilling softness. 'Then repeat the process at the end of the evening?' He waited a beat. 'You really believe I'd let that happen?'

He stripped off his briefs, then walked naked into the *en suite*.

Ana felt no satisfaction in the argument, and a wicked little imp urged her to march in there after him for the last word. Except there would be only one end, and she didn't have the time.

Instead she took a deep, steadying breath, and made her way downstairs, aware that Petros was waiting in the foyer.

'You get to play chauffeur.' She even managed a faint smile as she preceded him out to Luc's Mercedes.

'Luc has your best interests at heart.'

She slid into the front passenger seat, and waited until Petros slipped in behind the wheel. 'He's a dictatorial tyrant.'

The car eased forward and covered the distance to the gates. 'You're the wife of a wealthy man who prefers to implement precautions, rather than dismiss them and take unnecessary risks.'

'So shut up, and dance to the puppeteer's tune?'

'Some would be grateful.'

'This particular *someone* doesn't like being given orders.'

He entered New South Head Road. 'Where to, in the city, Ms Dimitriades?'

The irony was they weren't meeting in the city, but at Double Bay, and she named the restaurant, thanked him when he drew to a halt immediately outside it, then stepped into the plush entrance.

Her father and Rebekah were already seated at a table, and she greeted them with affection, then she requested mineral water and perused the menu.

'I've put the sale of my apartment in the hands of an agent, and I fly out to New York tomorrow,' William Stanford revealed when the waiter had taken their orders.

Rebekah threw questions thick and fast, and it was evident their father's answers failed to satisfy.

When William settled the bill, indicating the need to leave in order to pack, Rebekah summoned the waiter for tea and coffee, querying as soon as it arrived, 'You already knew, didn't you?'

'The possibility of New York, yes,' Ana stressed carefully.

'Why this sudden move? And I don't buy the necessity to sell the apartment.' Her eyes narrowed. 'He's in some kind of trouble. At a guess, Luc's involved, which means it's something to do with the bank.' Her lips pursed, then thinned to a grim line. 'Suppose you tell me the truth. All of it. Not just what you think I should hear.'

The telling was virtually a verbatim explanation of what William Stanford had confided over lunch.

'Just assure me you played no part in Luc's decision not to prosecute,' Rebekah pleaded. 'I'd kill him if I thought he'd dragged you back into a marriage you'd decided you no longer wanted.'

She was too clever by half. 'I wanted a break from Celine's tiresome behaviour.'

'And that's it? All of it?'

It was all she could bring herself to admit, and she resisted the childish urge to cross her fingers behind her back to minimise the lie. 'Yes.'

Something jogged her memory. 'I almost forgot. Luc suggested you join us for dinner Monday night.'

'Kind of him. Persuade Petros to serve moussaka and I'll bring him flowers.'

'I've no idea whether Luc plans eating out or at home. I'll ask and let you know. There's just one more thing...Jace will be there.'

'No.' Rebekah's response was immediate and adamant.

'*No*, because it's Jace? Or no, end-of-story?' Ana queried, and saw Rebekah's mouth thin.

'I can't stand the man.'

'Because he rubs you up the wrong way?' There was more to this than she thought. Rebekah had met him during one of his previous visits to Sydney, but they hadn't dated...at least, not that she was aware.

'That's the understatement of the year,' her sister growled, and Ana felt bound to ask,

'Don't you wonder *why*?'

'Oh, yes, sister dear.' Her voice held bitterness. 'I know precisely why. I just don't care to explore it.'

Ana was silent for a few seconds as she carefully weighed her words. 'Maybe you should.'

Rebekah speared her with a killing glare. 'Don't play amateur psychologist.'

'That wasn't my intention.'

'Oh, dammit.' Rebekah appeared contrite, for she hadn't meant to overreact. 'I'll come to dinner. It'll give me the utmost satisfaction to put Jace Dimitriades in his place.'

Tiredness crept over her, which, combined with the events of the day, resulted in the need to bring the evening to an end. 'I'll call a cab.' She extracted her cellphone and keyed in the necessary digits.

'You didn't drive in?' At her sister's faint grimace she indicated, 'I'll drop you home.'

She did, and Luc was waiting at the door as Rebekah brought her car to a halt.

'Your guardian angel.' She leaned forward and brushed a light kiss to Ana's cheek. 'I'll see you in the morning. And thanks.'

'For what?'

'Being you.'

Ana slid out from the car, waved as Rebekah eased the car forward, then she entered the foyer and met Luc's dark scrutiny.

'I was waiting for your call.' There was silk threading his voice.

'Why, when Rebekah offered to drop me home?' she asked reasonably.

'It's late.'

'We stayed on to talk a while.'

He took in her pale features, the faint smudges beneath her eyes. 'You should have ended the evening before this.'

'Don't,' she warned. 'Tell me something I already know.' The events of the day, Celine, a vivid reminder of William Stanford's folly, being less than totally honest with Rebekah...all seemed to manifest itself into a blazing headache. Add tiredness, and it wasn't an enviable combination.

'Go on up to bed. Can I bring you anything?'

She wanted to say 'Just *you*'. As it used to be, before Celine reappeared on the scene. But the words never left her lips, and she shook her head, feeling almost undone by the underlying care apparent.

She would have given anything to believe it was for her alone, and not because of the child she nurtured in her womb.

He set the security system, and doused the lights, then he followed her upstairs to their room, slipping out of the jeans and polo shirt he'd donned after his shower.

They both slid into bed at the same time, and he snapped off the bedside light, then gathered her close.

He dealt with her faint protest by closing his mouth over her own, sweeping his tongue in an evocative tasting that made him want more, much more, and he shaped her lissom body with his hands, aware of the slight tenderness of her breasts, the quivering response as he trailed an exploratory path over her stomach to the sensitive apex at the top of her thighs.

He pleasured her with such acute sensitivity it was all she could do not to cry out as sensuality reached fever pitch, and she clung to him, urging his possession until he joined his body to her own.

His mouth covered her own as they scaled the heights of passion in a rhythm only lovers shared.

Afterwards she fell asleep in his arms, and she had no knowledge that the man who held her lay awake in the darkness, lost in reflective thought.

CHAPTER SEVEN

ANA followed the delivery van into the bowels of Celine's apartment building, and secured the lift while Harry, the delivery guy, transported the buckets of cut flowers.

'That's everything, Harry?'

'The lot.'

'OK, let's go.'

Harry did the heavy work, then left, and Ana utilised the laundry as her work-station.

'I trust you won't make a mess.'

Ana glanced up from separating various stands of natives, and aimed for a pleasant smile. 'It'll be minimal, Celine, and contained here.'

A half-hour should have been sufficient, but it took twice that as Celine changed her mind on previously agreed displays.

If Ana had been mean-spirited, she would have said it was a deliberate attempt to minimise her ability and expertise.

She silently repeated 'the customer is always right' mantra, and maintained a professionally polite demeanour. But it was difficult, very difficult!

At last all three displays finally earned Celine's

grudging approval, and Ana began restoring the laundry to its former tidiness.

It didn't take long, and she emerged into the hallway, empty buckets in hand, her equipment neatly stacked in a holdall.

'Watch your back, darling,' Celine advised coolly as she led the way to the door. 'I play to win.'

'And you don't care who you hurt in the process?'

The woman plucked an imaginary speck from the sleeve of her blouse. 'Not at all.'

'Naturally, Luc is the prize.'

'Of course.'

'You've neglected one aspect in your campaign,' Ana said carefully.

'And what's that?'

'Luc's willingness to play.'

'You don't get it, do you?' Celine queried. 'Men of Luc's calibre think nothing of maintaining a mistress.'

'While the wife turns a blind eye, accepting the lifestyle, social prestige, and unlimited spending money in lieu of fidelity?'

'You could do much worse.'

'Sorry, Celine. That's not what I want for myself or my child.'

A concerted smile tilted Celine's carefully painted mouth. 'Can I take that as a given?'

'Absolutely.'

It wasn't the best exit line she'd ever offered, but she derived a sense of dignity as she walked from the apartment and took the lift down to the basement carpark.

It was late when she arrived home. Luc's Mercedes wasn't in the garage, and when she checked her cellphone there was a text message relaying a business meeting had run over time and they intended winding it up over dinner.

A message Petros confirmed as she made her way through the foyer to the kitchen.

'I've made vegetable soup, with a steak salad.'

Oliver appeared through the doorway and stalked across the tiles to brush himself against her leg. She bent down and scratched behind his ear, then stroked his tummy when he rolled over onto his back.

'I'll go shower and change, then be down in about fifteen minutes.'

Tonight she chose to eat indoors, and afterwards she settled down in front of the television set, channel-hopped, then riffled through the collection of DVDs, found one that appealed, and slotted it into the player.

At nine Petros brought her freshly made tea, then he retired to his flat.

The movie ran its course, and she wavered between slotting in another or going to bed.

Bed won, and she settled Oliver in the laundry, then made her way upstairs.

She reflected on the day's events as she discarded her clothes, lingering on Celine's pernickety fussing with the floral displays. A dinner party. She wondered how it was going, and who were the guests.

Then her hands froze.

No. Surely not. Luc's *business meeting* was a legitimate meeting…wasn't it? He wouldn't, couldn't be one of Celine's dinner guests. *Could he?*

However, the seed of doubt was planted, and steadily over the next hour it took root.

Imagination was a terrible thing, Ana accepted as she plumped her pillow for the umpteenth time and checked the bedside clock.

Eleven-o-five. So it was a leisurely meal, with Luc and his associates lingering over coffee.

She was still awake at eleven-thirty, convinced the business meeting was long over…if in fact there had been any meeting at all!

Damn Luc. If he'd dined as a guest at Celine's apartment, she'd kill him. In her mind, she conducted the argument they would have, the accusations she'd fling, and the physical fight that would follow. Then, she reasoned, she'd throw a few clothes into a suitcase and walk out of this house, his life, and never return.

Luc Dimitriades would never see his child, never again see *her*, and…

The peal of the telephone was a stark, intrusive sound that jolted her into action, and she fumbled for the bedside lamp, then picked up the receiver.

'Luc?'

'He'll be home soon, darling.' Celine's voice was

recognisable and held a distinct purr. 'Just thought I'd let you know.'

Ana heard a click as the call ended, and she slowly lowered the receiver down onto its cradle.

A few choice oaths slipped from her tongue as she stared blankly at the opposite wall. *Bastard.* How could he?

All too easily, she concluded silently.

She switched off the lamp and settled down in bed to stare emptily into the room's darkness for what seemed an age.

Images ran through her mind. Luc sharing Celine's table, conversing with fellow guests. A cynical laugh rose in her throat. Or maybe there were no guests at all, and it was strictly dinner *à deux.*

And afterwards... Dear heaven, she didn't want to think about *afterwards.*

He'd promised fidelity. Would he, *had* he broken that promise?

Get real, a tiny voice taunted. As if he's going to admit to it.

A slight sound made the breath catch in her throat, and she tensed as the bedroom door opened, then closed with an almost silent click.

He didn't turn on a light, and seconds later she heard the faint rustle of clothes being discarded. He'd probably shrugged out of his jacket and loosened his tie as he ascended the stairs, and it wasn't difficult to picture him unbuttoning his shirt, pulling it free from his trousers and tossing it onto the bedroom chair.

Shoes and socks would follow, and she detected the slide of a zip fastener as he prepared to remove his trousers.

All that remained were his briefs, and they too would be discarded to suit his preference to sleep naked.

For a moment she had a mental image of his tall, tightly muscled frame. The breadth of shoulder, the tapered waist, lean hips, powerful thighs. The fluid way he moved.

The mere thought he might have been at Celine's apartment incensed her, and her body tensed as she felt the faint depression of the mattress.

If he came close… Her mind seethed with a number of possible scenarios, each featuring various forms of retribution.

For the space of a few seemingly long seconds it seemed as if he was settling to sleep, and she slowly released the breath she'd unconsciously held from the moment he'd slid into bed.

The brush of his thigh and the touch of his arm as he curled his large body into the curve of her own brought an instant reaction.

Ana jabbed her elbow into his ribcage in a stark movement that took him completely by surprise, and the breath hissed from his throat as she kicked both heels into his shins.

'Don't you *dare* touch me!' The words scarcely

left her mouth when she followed them with a scandalised yelp as he used both arms to hold her close. 'Let me go, damn you!'

He was too big, too strong, for her to escape, and any attempt she made to kick his shins was prevented as he scissored both her legs between his own.

In one easy movement he rolled onto his back, carrying her with him, holding her there with galling ease as he reached out a hand and switched on the bedside light.

She looked magnificent in her fury, Luc perceived through narrowed eyes. Her hair was loose and tumbled, her cheeks flushed, her eyes brilliant sapphire shards meant to tear him to shreds.

The nightshirt she wore didn't begin to cover her and rode high over her hips.

'Now,' Luc growled huskily. 'Suppose you explain what this is all about.'

Ana struggled afresh, and managed to free one of her hands. She acted without thought, barely conscious of swinging her arm in a swift arc until her palm connected with his cheek. The sharp sound seemed loud in the silence of the room, and there was a part of her that registered horror at having lashed out at him.

Dear God. Such anger culminating in one retaliatory slap.

Her eyes widened in shock as she saw his features harden, facial muscles tightening into a visual mask of anger.

'Let me go!'

'Not in this lifetime, *pedhaki mou*.'

'You're hurting me.'

'No. I'm being extremely careful not to.' He had no trouble restraining her hands, and he was quick to take evasive action as she brought her head down and attempted to bite his arm. 'Stop it. You'll only hurt yourself.'

'Go to hell.'

'You consign me there with increasing regularity.' His voice was a hateful drawl that irked her unbearably. 'This isn't the first time I've had to attend a business dinner and arrived home late. Why such a reaction *tonight*?'

She wanted to hit him, and tried, only to find the effort futile. 'As if you don't know!'

His features bore a sculpted hardness, and his eyes were dark. Temper held in tight control, but there, none the less. 'If I knew, I wouldn't need to ask.'

Ana made a further attempt to pull free, and failed. 'I hate you.'

'For what, specifically?'

Her anger moved up a notch. 'This afternoon I spent an hour in Celine's apartment arranging flowers for a dinner party she was having tonight.' She threw him a fulminating glare. 'Twenty minutes ago she rang to tell me you were on your way home.'

Luc went still. 'You believe I was with Celine?' His voice was quiet. Way too quiet.

'You do the maths.'

'You think I'd lie to you?'

She didn't answer, couldn't. Her voice seemed to have temporarily disappeared.

'Worse,' he continued silkily. 'Come from her bed to yours?'

Icily bleak eyes riveted hers, trapping her in his gaze, and she caught the grim resolve apparent as he captured her head and held it fast.

'You expect me to accept your word unconditionally?'

'Is that so difficult?'

'Based on blind faith?' Ana lashed out with scepticism. 'My naïvety?' She was on a roll. 'Please. Don't insult my intelligence.'

He held on to his temper with difficulty. 'Why would I go out for hamburger when I have fillet steak at home?'

Oh, my. 'That's some analogy.'

'*Cristos.*' The oath held a dangerous softness that sent apprehension scudding down the length of her spine. 'This has gone far enough!'

In one fluid movement he slid from the bed and picked up the phone, then swore and crossed to the small antique desk, flicked on the lamp, then he opened a drawer and pulled out a phone book.

It took him only seconds to riffle through the pages, find the appropriate one, scan the relevant names and punch in the required digits.

Ana told herself she wasn't going to listen, but

she'd have had to put both hands over her ears to close out the sound of his voice.

Hard, inflexible words, with no hint of observing any social niceties, they carried an unmistakable warning to cease and desist from verbal stalking, or he'd take legal action.

His controlled anger held a menacing quality as he replaced the receiver and turned to face her.

'Give me all of it. From the beginning.'

'Celine?'

'*All*, Ana. Every hint, each accusation...don't leave anything out.'

It took a while, but at last she was done, and her face paled at his expression.

'That's it?'

Most of it...unless you counted the tone of voice, the malicious intent.

He wanted to pull on some clothes, collect his keys, drive to Celine's apartment and issue her with a writ. And while he had the power to get his lawyer out of bed, there was the due process of the law to observe, and no judge was going to comply at this hour of the night.

'You should have told me all this before.'

'I thought I had. Some of it,' she amended, and incurred his dark look.

'She won't bother you again.'

Want to bet? Somehow she doubted Celine would fade gracefully into the woodwork. Ana had blown her out of the water, and revenge would surely follow.

Luc slid into bed and gathered her close. 'Don't ever keep anything from me again.'

His mouth sought hers, and a hollow protest rose and died in her throat as he forced her jaw wide and plundered at will.

It became a ravaging assault on her senses, flagrant, primitive, and demanding, until he conquered each and every one of her defences.

Then, and only then, his mouth gentled fractionally and took on an eroticism she fought hard to resist.

Hungry, sensual, he caressed with devastating expertise, coaxing her capitulation until he sensed the moment she stopped fighting him.

One hand moved, catching the hem of her nightshirt before tugging it over her head, then he reached forward and began tracing the outline of her breast, watching her eyes dilate as sensation arched through her body.

Not content, he teased and tantalised the delicate peak before shifting to its twin, and she gasped as he spread his fingers and trailed a path to her waist.

Sensation spiralled through her body, and she made no protest as he brought his head down to hers in a kiss that drove her mindless.

With care he gathered her close and rolled over so their positions were reversed, then he eased into her, taking it slow as he controlled each plunge until she was driven almost mad with need.

In desperation she grazed her teeth over the hard muscle and sinew at his shoulder, then trailed low to one male nipple...and rendered a love-bite that brought the breath hissing between his teeth.

'So you want to play, hmm?'

It was she who groaned out loud as he took revenge in tantalising every pulse-beat, each sensory pleasure spot until she began to beg, and she cried out as he took her high, held her there, then caught her as she fell.

For a while she didn't want to move, didn't feel she could, and she rested in his arms, luxuriating in the slow drift of his fingers along the edge of her spine, soothing as his lips brushed her temple, then slipped to taste the delicate hollows at the base of her neck.

Minutes later he shifted her to one side, then slid to his feet and walked naked to the valet frame, collected his wallet, removed a credit slip from a leather sleeve, and handed it to her.

'The restaurant at the Ritz-Carlton Hotel. I picked up the tab for four.' He moved to the phone. 'You want I should ring Henri, the *maître d'*, and have him confirm what time we left?'

The date, the amount, both tallied. Irrefutable proof.

'I owe you an apology.' It wasn't easy to say the

words. It was even harder to look at him. But she did, and didn't let her gaze waver.

For someone as delusional and determined as Celine, it wouldn't have proven too difficult to discover Luc's plans and slip a waiter money to phone her when Luc left the restaurant.

'Accepted.'

CHAPTER EIGHT

ANA knew as soon as she hit the traffic snarl that she should have taken Rebekah's advice and left the shop earlier. Now she'd be impossibly late.

Dammit. Why *me*? she silently demanded of the Deity. Except no one was listening. The traffic remained stalled, and the only certainty was the knowledge she wouldn't be going anywhere in a hurry.

Luc *would not* be pleased. The evening's event was a prestigious fund-raiser, and the guest speaker a prominent American ex-president.

Everyone who was *anyone* would be there. Including Celine. But not, she prayed God, seated at the same table.

She checked the time, and hesitated between two options. Ring Luc from her cellphone, or wait for him to contact her.

Better make the call. He answered on the second peal, and the sound of his voice did strange things to her equilibrium.

It was damnable the effect he had on her, even from a distance. Elevated heartbeat, a faint breathlessness, and heat...the acute sexual awareness of shared intimacy. Past, present, future. She only had to think of him to have numerous erotic images flood her mind.

Get over it, she remonstrated silently.

'I won't say you should have left the shop before now.'

'Please don't. I'll be there whenever this line of traffic begins to move.'

It did, eventually, and she reached home with the sure knowledge it would take more than a miracle to shower, change, dress and *shine* in less than ten minutes.

She managed it in thirty, the scarlet bias-cut silk organza gown with its knee-high ruffled split a masterpiece of fabric and style. The simply cut bodice and shoestring straps completed a stunning design, complemented by her upswept hair, expertly applied make-up, and minimum jewellery.

Luc had been dressed when she first entered the bedroom, and now she bore his analytical scrutiny with a degree of uncertainty.

Was the gown too over-the-top? She'd fallen in love with it when she'd seen it displayed on a model. On impulse she'd extracted her credit card, added matching stiletto-heeled evening sandals and evening bag. Only to have reservations as to her sanity in expending so much on a single outfit.

'If you're aiming for the *wow* factor, you've achieved it.'

Success! She sent him a dazzling smile. 'Ah, a compliment.'

He looked stunning in anything he wore, for he exuded a certain intrinsic *something* that isolated him from other men. Difficult to pin down to any one thing, it was a combination of height and stature, the way he held himself and the way he moved. It was also the compelling quality that hinted at a raw primitiveness beneath the surface. The self-assurance of dynamic power, latent and devoid of arrogance…but there, none the less.

He would command attention in jeans and a sweatshirt. Attired in evening clothes, snowy-white shirt and black bow-tie, he was something else.

Her eyes held a wicked gleam. 'If I return it, you might get a swelled head.' She collected her evening bag, and gathered up a matching wrap. 'Shall we leave?'

'Yes.' He crossed to her side. 'But first—' He lowered his head, wanting, needing the taste of her, and his mouth captured hers in a kiss that tore the foundations of her composure…as he meant it to.

Reassurance…his, or hers? He told himself it was for her. And knew he lied.

The city hotel venue was crowded, the entrance brightly lit, a cavalcade of cars lined up waiting for valet parking, and there was security everywhere.

It took a while to get through the cordoned area, and by the time they reached the grand ballroom most everyone had passed through the doors and was seated.

Photographers were busy capturing the *crème de*

la crème of the rich and famous for the society pages of leading newspapers and national magazines.

It was, Ana perceived, *smile* time. Glitz and glamour, expensive jewellery, the drift of exotic perfumes meshed with the buzz of conversation as Luc caught hold of her hand and led the way to their reserved table.

They slipped into their seats just as centre lights dimmed and the MC began his opening speech outlining the charity's achievements, their projections for the coming year, and the specific purpose for this evening's gala event.

Waiters moved unobtrusively, weaving with precision through the many tables as they delivered starters, and wine stewards hovered attentively.

From where they were seated it was possible to see the VIP table, and she caught a glimpse of the ex-president, the silver, almost white, well-groomed hair, the lightly tanned complexion, the easy smile.

Conversation at their own table was interesting and varied, and she was supremely conscious of Luc seated at her side.

Last night… *Don't go there*, an inner voice cautioned. It was difficult not to recall her anger, the rage, and her reaction. She'd never physically hit anyone in her life. The thought she'd attempted to strike him appalled her.

All day she'd managed to put it to one side as she became caught up with a rush of orders and customers.

Now, she found her attention being drawn back to the accusations she'd flung at him…and the result.

How was it possible to *hate* someone one moment, be filled with contrition the next, then participate in lovemaking as if nothing mattered except the moment?

It was like riding a crazy emotional roller coaster.

'Amazing man, isn't he? No one would imagine from looking at him that he once held the fate of a nation in his hands.' The guest leaned in close. 'Apart from our state premier, everyone else at his table is security.'

'I imagine security men and women are evenly spread throughout the room,' Ana inclined politely.

She was spared from further comment as the state premier was introduced and the waiter began removing plates.

At the conclusion of the main course, Ana quietly slipped from her seat and went in search of the powder room. She was one of several women in need of the facilities, and afterwards she took a minute in front of the mirror to freshen her lipstick.

'Don't go crying to Luc again, darling.'

Celine, and on a mission. With no doubt as to the target.

'What makes you think I did?'

'Oh, *please*. Luc and I have no secrets from each other.'

Did her hand shake? She hoped not. 'Don't you have anything better to do?'

'Than *what*, precisely?'

'Meddle in other people's lives. Mine, in particular.'

'I can't believe I'm not getting through to you.'

'Oh, you are, Celine,' she assured. 'Loud and clear.' She paused a beat. 'Pity it's such a waste of your time and energy.'

'Luc is—'

'Free to choose, Celine.' The emphasis was deliberate. 'It would appear he's chosen me.'

The other woman's expression was scathing. 'Simply because you wear his ring and carry his child? Darling, how naïve are you?'

She slid the capped lipstick tube into her evening bag and turned away from the mirrored wall. 'I have nothing further to say to you.' She moved back a step, only to pause as the other woman caught hold of her wrist. 'Take your hand off me.'

'I could point out a number of successful businessmen whose wives turn a blind eye to their husbands' indiscretions.'

'I'm not one of them.' Calm, she had to remain calm. If she lost her temper, this debacle would digress into a physical cat fight.

Celine's lacquered nails bit into Ana's arm. 'Luc rang today and warned he wouldn't be able to see me for a while because you were making things difficult.' Her smile held a vindictiveness that was vaguely frightening. 'Not a wise move, darling.'

She'd had enough. 'Keep this up, Celine, and you'll have charges laid against you.'

Celine rendered a vicious pinch, then flung Ana's arm wide. 'Luc would never allow it.'

Ana moved towards the door, then paused. 'Perhaps now would be a good time to tell you I was in the room when Luc rang you last night.' She walked into the carpeted foyer and re-entered the ballroom.

The ex-president had already begun his speech, and Luc shot her a studied glance as she slipped into her seat, then returned his attention to the man at the podium.

The speech concluded amid enthusiastic applause, then the lights brightened and the waiters busied themselves serving the dessert and coffee.

'Are you OK?'

Now, there was a question. 'Solicitous attention, Luc?'

'Let me guess,' he drawled. 'Celine bailed you up in the powder room?'

'Got it in one.'

'Whereupon you told her to get lost, and she retaliated?'

'Ah, you possess psychic powers.'

'Damage control is—'

'Something at which you excel.' She hadn't meant to sound bitter, and she saw his gaze sharpen.

He caught hold of her hand and linked her fingers through his own, holding them firmly when she endeavoured to pull free.

'We dealt with this last night.'

'Did we? I thought we just had sex.'

'That, too.'

The waiter placed cups and saucers onto the table, and she indicated tea in preference to coffee.

'I'll take you home.'

'I don't want to leave yet.' Her gaze was remarkably clear. 'And escape isn't the answer.'

'Nor is a heated argument in public,' he accorded drily, and she arched one delicate brow.

'Is that what we're about to have?'

'Count on it.'

Ana picked up an extra tube of sugar, broke it and stirred the contents into her tea. 'Energy for the fight.'

'Don't push me too far.'

She proffered a deliberately sweet smile. 'I'm shaking.'

'So brave.'

His faint mockery brought a surge of anger. 'What can you do to me that you haven't done already?'

Something shifted in his eyes, and she felt a trickle of apprehension slither down her spine. 'Careful, *pedhi mou.*'

It seemed pointless to further the civility façade, and she sipped her tea, indulged in animated conversation with a fellow guest, then became the epitome of politeness when Luc indicated they should leave.

Her face ached from the smile she kept in place

as they paused at one table and another to talk with friends and acquaintances, and she stood silently at the hotel entrance as the valet called up their car.

Ana didn't offer a word during the drive to Vaucluse, and once inside the house she made straight for the stairs.

Luc re-set the security alarm and entered their suite as she tried unsuccessfully to release the clasp fastening the slender gold chain circling her throat.

He shrugged out of his jacket, undid his tie, loosened his shirt buttons, then crossed to her side.

'Let me try.'

His fingers were warm against her nape, and she wanted to sweep away from him. Except what good would it do except exacerbate an already volatile situation?

He freed the clasp in seconds, then turned her round to face him.

'You want to fight, or do we call a truce?'

Vengeance tinged her voice. 'Fight.'

'Then throw the first punch.'

She made a fist and aimed for his chest, felt it connect against hard muscle and sinew…and bruised her knuckles.

'Your knees are supposed to buckle as you sink to the floor.'

'Want to try again?'

He was amused, damn him. She gave him a baleful glare as she nursed her hand. 'Not particularly.'

He smoothed his palms over her shoulders, slipping the straps free, then he tended to the zip fastening her gown.

The red silk organza slid to the carpet in a heap. All she wore were thong briefs and stiletto heels, and his breath caught in his throat at the beautiful symmetry of her slender curves.

Pale, satin-smooth skin, firm breasts, a slim waist, toned thighs.

He had an unrelenting urge to touch her, shape those curves with his hands, taste her. And when he was done, bury himself inside her, absorb her shuddering climax, then climb the heights with her and share a mutual shattering of the senses.

Luc reached out and cupped her face, then he lowered his mouth down over hers…and gave a grunt as her fist executed a stunning hook just beneath his ribcage.

'I think that's known as the element of surprise?'

His retribution was swift, and she gasped as he lifted her up against him and hooked her legs around his waist.

She felt him toe off one shoe, then the other, and he shifted her higher as he dealt with his belt, his trousers. His shirt was wrenched off and tossed to the floor, then he stood looking at her, his features raw with something intensely primitive.

The heat and hardness of his arousal pushed against the scrap of silk covering the apex of her thighs, and in one smooth movement he slid his fingers beneath the thin strap and disposed of it.

Dear heaven. There was nothing measured or controlled about him. Only electrifying passion and a fierce need for consummation.

Ana waited for the moment he would plunge deep inside, and felt her eyes begin to glaze over as he rocked her slowly against him, exposing her clitoris to the satin-smooth hardness of his shaft.

'Luc—' She could barely speak as sensation exploded in an upward spiral that had her moaning out loud.

Just as she thought she could bear it no longer he walked to the bed and tumbled them both down onto the mattress.

Now. Did she cry it out? She couldn't be sure, and she groaned when he covered her mouth with his own in a kiss that duplicated the sexual act itself.

She reached for him, and he evaded her touch, choosing instead to trail a path to her breast where he savoured one tender peak before rendering attention to its twin, suckling there until she cried out with a mixture of pleasure and pain.

Not content, he moved low over her navel, then traced a tortuously slow path to render the most intimate kiss of all.

He wanted to have her beg for his possession, to feel the hunger, the want, and *need* him as much as he needed her.

The passion was mesmeric, *magical*. Too much. Way too much and beyond her control. Slow, silent tears trickled down over her temple and became lost in her hair as she tossed her head from one side to the other as she craved a release only he could give.

Her body shuddered in reaction, and he raised his head, saw the devastation etched on her features, then he shifted to close his mouth over hers in an evocative kiss that made her want to weep afresh.

It was then he slid into her, taking care with long, slow strokes that culminated in an explosive crescendo.

Afterwards he pulled up the covers and held her close, trailing a light, feathery path along her spine in a soothing gesture until her breathing steadied to an even beat.

'Rise and shine.'

Ana registered Luc's voice, the words, and opened her eyes a fraction.

It was Sunday morning, she didn't need to go into the shop, and she had no particular inclination to get out of bed at…she took a moment to check the time…eight o'clock.

She spared him a glance, and saw he'd already showered and was dressed in casual jeans and a polo shirt. He looked vital, and far too lethally male for any woman's peace of mind. Especially at this early hour.

'You'd better have a good reason for suggesting I *rise* and *shine*.'

Luc indicated the tray resting on the bedside pedestal. 'Tea and toast. Fruit.'

She slid into a sitting position, realised she wasn't wearing a thing and pulled the sheet high. '*You* made this?'

He sat down on the edge of the bed. 'Don't sound so surprised.'

'Thank you.' Her lips curved into a slight smile. 'Presumably you want to get me out of bed, rather than keep me in it…so what gives?'

'I plan to take the boat out onto the harbour for the day.'

Given the *boat* was a luxury cruiser moored at a marina, he'd obviously planned ahead. She had to ask. 'Are you inviting anyone else along?'

'No.'

Better and better. 'What time do you want to leave?'

'As soon as you're ready.'

She looked beautifully tousled, her skin flushed from sleep, her eyes deep and lustrous. He reached forward and pushed a wayward lock of hair behind her ear.

There was a need to spend time with her, in order to help repair some of the damage caused by Celine's interference.

'Are you going to sit there and watch me eat?'

He looked completely relaxed, although even at ease there was a leashed quality evident. A sensual element that never failed to stir her emotions.

'I've already had breakfast.'

She finished the tea and toast, then peeled the banana and ate it. 'I need to shower.'

He caught up her silk wrap and handed it to her. 'I'll see you downstairs. Twenty minutes?'

She made it in fifteen, choosing jeans and a knit top over a bikini, and she'd snagged a sweater in case of a cool breeze.

The skies were an azure blue with hardly a cloud in sight, and there was warmth in the early-summer sun as they gained the large marina.

After a hectic week, the prospect of cruising the harbour seemed an idyllic way to spend the day. Luc's cruiser was a sleek-looking craft with gleaming white paint, expensive fittings, and contained a roomy cabin, master suite and bathroom.

Within minutes of boarding Luc started the engines, then eased the craft out into open waters. Ana stood at his side, admiring the rocky promontories where beautiful harbour-side mansions dotted the landscape, the numerous coves and bays.

Craft in varying shapes and sizes were out on the harbour, some with definite destinations in mind, others just idly exploring the waterways or putting down anchor to try their luck at fishing.

The muted sound of the powerful engines was a pleasant background noise. 'Are you meeting Jace at the airport?'

Luc spared her a quick glance. 'His flight gets in late. He'll take a cab to the hotel and call me in the morning.'

There were questions she wanted to ask, and she struggled with them, not willing to spoil the day or upset the delicately balanced truce they shared.

The sun rose higher in the sky, dappling the waters with reflected light, and around midday Luc cut the engines and dropped anchor.

'Lunch. Do you want to eat in the cabin, or outside?'

'Outside,' Ana said without hesitation, and took bottled drinks from the cabin refrigerator while Luc unpacked the large chilled cooler.

Petros had been busy, she perceived as she checked out roast chicken, succulent ham, various salads, fresh bread rolls and fruit. It was a feast, and she set it out on plates, added cutlery, then sank onto one of the cushioned squabs.

Luc settled down opposite and layered a roll with chicken and salad, then bit into it with evident enjoyment.

Ana followed suit, reflecting a week ago she'd been in a different place, endeavouring to sort out a wealth of ambivalent emotions.

Would Luc have come after her if he hadn't discovered she was pregnant? And if she'd demanded a divorce, would he have insisted on a reconciliation, or merely called his lawyer?

She wanted to know the answers, but she didn't have the courage to ask the questions. What if the answers Luc gave weren't what she wanted to hear?

Did he care for her, *really* care for her? Or was she merely a convenient wife who suited his needs?

In bed, they were in perfect accord. Out of it, she spent time trying to convince herself she should be content with the status quo.

A week ago, she'd thought she had choices and options. Now they'd been taken away from her.

'I value what is mine. That's a given.'

Value wasn't *love*, she added silently. Would he have followed her to the Coast if she hadn't been pregnant?

'Yes.'

Her eyes widened beneath the tinted lens of her sunglasses. 'You read minds?'

'You have expressive features. *Yes*...I would have hauled you back to Sydney.' He paused fractionally. 'And no,' he continued with chilling softness. 'Not solely because I discovered you carry our child. Or as some form of misguided revenge for your father's misappropriation of bank funds.'

Dared she believe him? She wanted to, desperately. The repetitive beep of a cellphone was an intrusion, and it took a few seconds to realise it was her own. The caller ID wasn't one she recognised, and there was surprised relief as she read a text message from her father confirming his safe arrival in New York together with the name of his hotel.

Ana put a call through to Rebekah and relayed the news, then she cleared away the remains of their lunch while Luc fired up the engines and headed south towards Botany Bay.

It was so warm, she stripped down to her bikini, took time to cover every exposed inch of skin with sun-screen lotion, then she spread out a towel and let the sun and fresh salt air work their soporific magic.

She must have dozed, for when she woke the sun had moved lower in the sky. It was still warm, but she sat up and pulled on the knit top, then rose to her feet.

The engines were silent, and she saw Luc sprawled comfortably at ease near by, reading a novel.

At that moment he glanced up and discarded the book. 'Ready to go home?'

'Yes. Thank you,' she added with sincerity.

Humour tugged the edges of his mouth. 'For what, specifically?'

'Organising the day.'

'My pleasure. We'll go out somewhere later for dinner.'

The thought of dressing up didn't appeal. 'Why not collect take-out and eat at home?'

'Anything in particular?'

Crispy noodles, heaps of vegetables, prawns and rice. 'Chinese?'

'Done.'

She looked at him in surprise. 'You're not going to override me?'

'Why would I do that?' he queried, and caught the gleam in her eyes as she laughed.

'You're being indulgent.'

'Is that such a terrible thing?' His light, teasing drawl brought an answering smile to her lips.

She could almost imagine they had taken a step back in time to the early days of their marriage, only to dismiss the thought as being fanciful. Yet there was a part of her that wanted what they once shared…the affection, fun, the spontaneity. The uninhibited loving, when there had been no doubts and she retained few insecurities.

It was almost six when they left the marina. Luc stopped *en route* to Vaucluse and picked up Chinese take-out, which they ate with chopsticks directly out of containers seated at a table on the terrace. Oliver sat close by, eager with expectancy for the occasional morsel of food.

Afterwards they watched the sunset, the brilliant flaring of orange streaked with pink and purple, followed by the gradual fading of colour with the onset of dusk.

It had been a near-perfect day, and she was reluctant to have it end. Tomorrow would see a return to work, and in the evening they were due to dine out with Jace and Rebekah.

Let's not forget Celine, Ana accorded silently on the edge of sleep. The woman was bound to wreak more havoc, given half a chance.

CHAPTER NINE

MONDAY was busy, orders flowed in, and what breaks Ana and Rebekah were able to take were minimal.

Consequently, it was almost six before they were able to get away from the shop, and traffic seemed even slower than usual as Ana headed for Vaucluse.

Luc pulled into the driveway seconds ahead of her, and she followed the Mercedes into the garage, parked, then slid from the car.

'You're late.'

There was disapproval in his tone, and Ana flashed him a stunning smile. 'Well, *hell*, so are you.'

She thought she caught a glimpse of humour in those dark eyes as she drew level, and her lips parted in surprise as he slid a hand beneath her nape and pulled her close.

'You have a sassy mouth.'

His head descended, and she was powerless to prevent the firm pressure of his mouth on hers as he bestowed an evocative kiss that left her wanting more.

'What was that for?'

He traced the fullness of her lower lip with an idle finger. 'Because I felt like it.'

Dear heaven, did he have any idea what he did to her? In bed, without a doubt. But out of it? Just the thought of him sent the blood coursing through her veins. Sexual chemistry, she perceived, was a powerful entity.

And *love*? To find a soul mate and gift one's heart unconditionally…to have the gift returned… Was it unattainable in life's reality? Or did that kind of love only exist in romantic fantasy?

There were times in the depths of passion, she thought it was possible. Except in the dark of night it was all too easy to believe the touch of a man's hands, the feel of his mouth, meant much more than it did. And without the words…

Although better no words, than a meaningless avowal that would only leave emptiness.

Get a grip, Ana berated silently. You knew when you married him that love wasn't part of the deal. Why should anything have changed? Except in the deepest recess of her heart she'd hoped that it might.

'What's going on in that head of yours, hmm?'

She blinked at the sound of his voice, and switched from passive reflection to the present in an instant.

'Contemplating how Jace and Rebekah will react to each other,' she declared with a blandness that didn't deceive him in the slightest.

Luc curved an arm over her shoulders as they made their way towards the foyer. 'I have no doubt Jace will handle her without much effort.'

As you handle me? Aloud, she retaliated, 'Rebekah wouldn't agree with you.'

Ana ascended the stairs as Luc paused to consult with Petros, and she began discarding clothes as soon as she entered the bedroom. Thirty minutes in which to shower, wash and dry her hair, dress and be ready to depart the house didn't allow for leisurely preparations.

The sound of cascading water masked the faint snick of the shower door opening, and she gave a startled gasp as Luc entered the cubicle.

'What do you think you're doing?'

He took the bottle of shampoo from her hand and poured a liberal quantity into his palm, then began massaging it into her hair.

'Indulging you.'

His drawling tone curled around her nerve-ends and tugged a little. 'I don't need you to indulge me,' she said fiercely, endeavouring to ignore the pleasure spiralling through her body. God, that felt good, so good!

His hands moved to her nape, then worked magic on her neck and shoulders. An appreciative sigh escaped her lips, and she felt the warmth within slowly build to a burning heat.

Luc rinsed the suds from her hair, smoothed back the wet length, then he lowered his mouth over hers in a soft, evocative kiss that had her leaning in to him, wanting, needing so much more.

His arousal was a potent, virile force, and she

whimpered a little as he eased back a little, gentling the kiss until his lips were just brushing hers. Then he held her at arm's length, and let his gaze roam over her slender form.

The thought of their child swelling her body almost brought him undone. The beauty of it, the miracle...

Already he could see the slight difference in the shape of her breasts, the aureoles, and he traced each contour and lightly cupped their weight, exalting in her faint intake of breath as he brushed each tender nub with his thumb.

He let one hand slip down to cover her waist, and wondered how long it would be before it began to thicken. A few more weeks...longer?

'Luc—'

'I want to look at you,' he said gently.

'Don't...' It was a token protest, for there was something magical happening here. Surely she could be forgiven for wanting to capture and hold the moment.

'Don't *what*?'

She made a last-ditch attempt at sensibility. 'We'll be late.'

His smile held musing humour. 'So, we'll be late.'

'Rebekah will never forgive me.' She gave a husky groan as his hand slid low over her abdomen and sought the sensitive clitoris. All it took was the glide of his fingers, and she became lost...*his*.

He lifted her easily, and she wrapped her legs

around his waist, then sank into him, loving the slow slick slide as she accepted his length.

Her mouth angled in to his, and she felt she was drowning, awash in libidinous sensation as his tongue tangled with hers in an oral simulation of the sexual act itself.

It was he who controlled the rhythmic pacing, its depth of penetration, and he cradled her as she climbed the heights, then caught her as she fell.

Like this, nothing else mattered. Only the man, the moment. It was possible to believe everything in her world was OK. No intrusions, no designing ex-mistress, and no nebulous ghost of his first wife to cloud the perfection of what they'd just shared.

Later there would be a reality check. But for now he was hers...in body, and affection. Was it so wrong to want it all? His heart, his soul?

Ana told herself she should be content with the positives...she was his wife, she was carrying their child.

The negative was Celine, who'd stop at nothing to cause trouble.

And then there was Emma, who'd occupied a brief part of his life before leaving it. In all honesty, she could hardly begrudge him the memory, and didn't.

It was almost eight when they entered the restaurant, and Ana sensed the tension apparent before she even reached their table.

'Ana.' Jace rose to his feet and greeted her with an affectionate hug, brushed his lips to each cheek in turn, then held her at arm's length. 'You are beautiful, *pedhaki mou*. I swear, if you were not already married to my cousin, I'd have no compunction in stealing you away.' His dark eyes held a devilish twinkle. 'If he dares to mistreat you, I promise to kill him.'

'Flatterer.' She offered him a winsome smile, then slid into the chair the waiter held out for her.

The resemblance between the two cousins was notable in that they shared the height, the breadth of shoulder, the dark, attractive good looks of their heritage. Add power, a dangerous alchemy, and it became a combustible combination.

How many years separated them? One, two? It could only be a few.

'You knew I didn't want to be with Jace one-on-one,' Rebekah remonstrated quietly as Luc and Jace perused the selection of wines.

'I'm sure you managed OK.' Given the thoughtful and rather musing expression Jace wore, it wasn't difficult to imagine he'd succeeded in getting beneath Rebekah's skin.

The waiter presented the menu, and they ordered a starter followed by a main, waived dessert in favour of the cheeseboard.

'So tell me how it is with the florist industry,' Jace drawled, and his eyes were watchful, sharp, beneath an indolent demeanour.

'I've been away for a few weeks,' Ana said lightly. 'Rebekah can expound on it.'

'To what purpose? I doubt Jace's interest is genuine.'

'On the contrary. I'm very interested in everything you do.'

Oh, my, this was assuming all the portents of a verbal clash.

'Really?' Rebekah didn't appear to care, but Ana knew her sister too well. The question had to be whether Jace saw beneath the practised and protective façade.

'You want to hear a florist's day begins at four in the morning when she leaves for the city flower markets? If she arrives there later than five, all the quality blooms have already been bought.'

She held out her hands. 'These are the major tools of our trade.' She gave them a rueful glance. 'They're in water, they get cut, scratched, blistered, and retain permanent callouses. Gloves don't work, they're too unwieldy, and creams don't begin to repair the damage. Forget manicures and nail polish.' Her faint grimace held fleeting cynicism. 'You want more?'

'You've left out standing on your feet all day, and dealing with difficult customers. Deliveries that go to incorrect addresses?' Jace drawled quizzically.

Rebekah chose silence, although Ana knew it cost her.

The food was delectable, and they ate with enjoyment.

'How long are you staying in Sydney?' Ana queried, directing her attention to Jace, whose home base was a private residence in New York's fashionable Upper East Side.

'As long as it takes to wrap up a few property deals. Has Luc told you I intend dragging him down to Melbourne day after tomorrow?'

'Not yet.'

Jace's smile held devilish humour. 'Can you manage without him for a few nights?'

'Easily.'

Luc caught hold of her hand and brought it to his lips. 'You're supposed to say *no*.'

His dark eyes held a lazy warmth that was wholly sensual, and she felt the answering kick of her pulse as it quickened in pace.

'Really?'

Jace chuckled, and touched the rim of his wine glass to Ana's water goblet. 'Salute. I know of no other woman who would dare take Luc to task.'

'My wife delights in deflating my ego.'

'Count yourself fortunate, cousin.'

Ana caught Rebekah's expressive eye-roll, and steered the conversation onto safer ground. 'Let's do dinner and the movies while Luc is away.'

'Wednesday night?'

'Done.'

'Do I get to have a say?' Luc queried mildly.

'None whatsoever.'

'Have Petros drive you.'

'Don't be ridiculous.'

'I could invite myself to stay over,' Rebekah suggested.

'Better,' Luc acquiesced. 'Petros still gets to be chauffeur.'

'Remind me to hit you when we get home.' She made the threat sound amusing, but there was no humour in the glance she cast him.

'I'll look forward to it.'

She couldn't win, so why try? Except the banter kept things light, and Jace and Rebekah's presence made for a pleasant evening.

It was after ten when they left the restaurant and drove home. Traffic was minimal, ensuring there were no delays at controlled intersections, and the lull provided a pleasant reminder the day was almost done.

'What time are you leaving for Melbourne?'

'Eager to be rid of me, *pedhi mou*?'

'Must I answer that?'

Together they entered the house, and Ana climbed the stairs to the upper floor while Luc set the security alarm.

She was in bed and on the verge of sleep when he joined her, and she made no protest as he gathered her close.

His lips nuzzled the warm scented skin at the edge of her neck, then trailed a path up the sensitive cord to savour the lobe of her ear before tracing the line of her jaw.

She adored the feel of him, the hard muscle and

sinew, the shape and contours of a body that was wholly male.

He made her come alive, as no man ever had, and the blood sang in her veins, heating her skin and activating every nerve cell until all her senses meshed and she became one throbbing entity.

Great sex. The best. For a while she lost herself in sensual euphoria, totally enraptured by the man who held her heart and captured her soul.

Ana glanced up at the sound of the electronic door buzzer, and her lips parted to form a warm smile. 'Jace.' Her greeting held genuine affection as he crossed to the counter. 'How nice to see you.'

He leant forward and brushed his lips to her cheek. 'And you, Ana.'

'Is your visit business or pleasure?'

His dark eyes held humour. 'One could say both.'

'Rebekah has stepped out for a few minutes.'

'Then I shall wait.'

Her grin was unrepentant. 'Thought you might.'

'Am I that transparent?'

She tilted her head a little, pretending to consider his mocking query. 'You're a Dimitriades,' she answered lightly. 'Transparency isn't one of your traits. Playing the game *is*.' Her expression sobered. 'Take care with my sister.'

The amusement disappeared. 'Or else you'll come out fighting?'

'Count on it.'

'I consider myself duly warned.'

'I don't suppose you're going to give me any hint of your intentions?'

'No.'

'Damn.'

He lifted a hand and tucked a stray tendril of hair back behind her ear. 'I can see why my cousin put a ring on your finger.'

'And that would be?'

'To put you off-limits to other men.'

'He might care to remember I put a ring on *his* finger.'

His gaze sharpened. 'Problems, Ana?'

The telephone provided a welcome interruption, and she wrote down the verbal order, took credit-card details, then tended to a customer who walked in off the street.

Rebekah's return coincided with another telephone call, and Ana dealt with it, aware that Luc's cousin was intent on buying roses. At least two dozen, she determined as Rebekah gathered them together, then spread Cellophane paper on the work table and carefully positioned the blooms.

Just as Ana replaced the receiver, a man entered the shop, chose a prepared bouquet, then bought and paid for it.

Busy didn't begin to describe it, and Ana checked the orders that should be ready for the delivery guy to collect on the late-morning run, glanced at the wall clock, and continued with preparations.

Whatever was happening between Rebekah and Jace reached a conclusion, and she acknowledged his 'goodbye' with a smile and watched as he exited the shop.

'That man,' Rebekah vented quietly as she joined Ana at the work table.

'What about him?'

Rebekah consulted the order book, then retrieved tissue, Cellophane wrap, and skilfully selected carnations, baby's breath. Nimble fingers spread them into an artistic display, and she caught ribbon from a stand of varied ribbon rolls, cut off a length and tied it within seconds.

'He doesn't understand the word *no*.'

'Really?'

'Do you know what he just did?' Rebekah didn't wait for an answer. 'He bought three dozen roses, paid for them, wrote on a card, then handed them to me.'

'Such an unforgivable sin,' Ana declared, tongue-in-cheek, and incurred her sister's glare. 'What did the card say?'

'*"Dinner tonight. Seven."*'

'Naturally you're not going to go.'

'Of course not.'

'And you'll be out when he calls.'

'Got it in one.'

Ana put the completed bouquet to one side, perused the next order, and began assembling it. 'Maybe you should share dinner with him—'

'Are you insane?'

'And tell him exactly what you think of him,' she continued, ignoring Rebekah's interruption.

'If I didn't know you cared,' her sister declared with mocking cynicism, 'I could almost imagine you *want* me to go out with him.'

'Not all men are like Brad.'

'Yeah, sure. Well, excuse me, but I don't feel inclined to go through the bullshit just to find out.'

'Jace is—'

'Nice? Come on, sweetheart. Most men present a civil façade. At first,' she qualified. 'Then if you don't *deliver* you get called every name under the sun. Mr *nice guy* becomes the octopus from hell.' She drew in a deep breath and released it slowly. 'And I've never been one for indiscriminate sex just for the sake of scratching an itch.'

'So cocoon yourself in cotton wool and play it safe?'

'Yes.'

It was an adamant reply, expected, and one she chose not to pursue. 'OK.'

Rebekah slanted her sister a sharp glance. 'Just *OK*? No verbal lecture?'

'No.'

'Now you're pissing me off.'

'You want to fight...go fight with someone else.'

'Such as Jace? Over dinner?'

Ana hid a faint grimace as she observed the way

her sister plucked blooms from numerous tubs. 'The blooms don't deserve to suffer.'

'No, they don't.' Rebekah crossed to the counter and collected the bouquet of roses sitting there. 'These can go back into stock.'

'Jace has paid for them in good faith.'

'So? I should just leave them there?'

'Take them home.'

'The hell,' Rebekah declared inelegantly. '*You* take them home.'

'They were a gift to you.'

'They're going back into stock.'

Ana paused, then quietly offered, 'Don't allow a mistake in the past cloud your chance of happiness in the future.'

'With Jace Dimitriades? Are you nuts?'

'Jace, *personally*,' she pursued, 'or *any* man?'

Rebekah opened her mouth, then closed it again. 'Knowing what I went through with Brad, during and after the marriage, you're suggesting I dive into shark-infested waters again?'

'Sharks *bite*.'

'And you don't think Jace will?'

'If he does, I know you'll bite back.'

Rebekah threw up her hands, rolled her eyes in expressive disbelief, then burst into laughter. 'I give up!'

'Besides,' Ana ventured with a hint of devilry. 'If you bite, you might acquire a taste for him.'

'*Hah*. And the cow jumped over the moon.'

They were saved from further cynicism by the simultaneous peal of the telephone and the door buzzer.

Business, Ana conceded, took priority. But it didn't prevent the silent thought that Jace Dimitriades might be just who Rebekah needed to restore her faith in the male of the species.

It was mid-afternoon when Ana picked up her cellphone on the second ring, identified Luc's private number on-screen and activated the call.

'How do you feel about attending a movie première tonight?'

'We're talking gala event, or slipping quietly into a city theatre?'

'Fox Studios.'

Definitely *gala*.

'It slipped my mind until Caroline reminded me this morning.'

The ultra-efficient secretary who kept track of Luc's business and social diary.

'What time do we need to leave?'

'Seven. Petros will have dinner ready at six. Try not to be late.'

For once she managed to get away from the shop ahead of time. Largely due to Rebekah's prompting, and the help of their new assistant.

Choosing what to wear didn't present a dilemma, and she plucked a delightful multi-layered gown from its hanger, spread it on the bed, and paused to admire the brilliant mix of deep blue and peacock-green. A luminous thread made the colours shimmer beneath the light. Exquisite for evening wear, it highlighted her blonde hair and matched her eyes.

'What is the movie, and who are the lead actors?' Ana queried *en route* to the studios.

'The lead actress is an American-based Australian, so is the producer.'

Of course. She'd read about its upcoming release in numerous publicity slots on television. It promised to be colourful and amusing, as well as entertaining.

Parking wasn't a problem, and they joined fellow guests entering the auditorium. *Invitation only,* it was a glamorous event with several city socialites and notables attending.

Celine's presence was guaranteed. The only thing Ana could hope for was they were seated far apart.

Social mingling was a refined art, she mused as a fellow guest called Luc's name. There were pleasantries to exchange, the occasional opinion that touched on business…and the need to have instant recall of a host of names.

She had to hand it to Luc…he didn't appear to falter.

'You possess an awesome memory,' she murmured as they moved forward, and he cast her a musing look.

'It's an acquired skill.'

'Very much part of *business*.' She hadn't meant an edge of cynicism to creep in.

'An essential courtesy,' he elaborated, his gaze

sharpening as he caught the nervous slide of her fingers over the elegant beading of her evening bag.

'I can promise she won't get near you.' His voice was calm, unruffled, and Ana cast him a startled glance.

'You intend sticking to my side all night?'

A tinge of amusement momentarily softened his features. 'Like glue.'

'This could get interesting.'

His fingers threaded through her own. 'I'm counting on it.'

'United we stand?'

His expression sobered, and she caught a brief glimpse of the steely determination exigent. 'Yes.'

So his aim was to present *togetherness*. Just *how* together did he intend them to portray?

Very, Ana conceded, half an hour later. The light brush of his fingers down her arm; the arm loosely circling her waist; the way his fingers sought her nape and effected a brief, soothing massage there; the way his palm rested between her shoulder blades and moved fractionally.

It represented a tactile reassurance as they stood conversing with fellow guests, and there was a part of her that wished it was for real.

Her body felt alive with evocative sensation, and she was almost willing to swear she could feel the blood course through her veins, activating all her nerve-ends.

Was it possible to tune in to someone to such a

degree you felt you were meant to be like two halves of a whole? That only *this* person was your soul mate, never to be replaced by anyone else?

Love. Unconditional, abiding love. A gift without equal…beyond price. Reciprocal, it represented heaven on earth.

A light, fleeting touch to her lips caused her to start in surprise, and she was powerless to still the surge of emotion that rose from deep inside as she met Luc's unfathomable gaze.

For a moment she was acutely vulnerable, and she caught her lower lip with the edge of her teeth to prevent their faint tremor.

Had he glimpsed what she tried so desperately to hide?

His finger traced the curve, lingered at its edge, then he lowered his mouth to hers in a sweet evocative kiss that was all too brief.

She felt her eyes widen, and her voice emerged as a shaky whisper. 'What was that for?'

His smile completely disarmed her. 'Because I wanted to.'

Oh, my. For a few heightened seconds she wasn't conscious of anyone else. There was only Luc, and the moment.

Ana saw the inherent strength apparent, the integrity…and something else. Then it was gone, and she wondered if she'd imagined a quality beneath the slumbering passion evident.

Get a grip, she cautioned silently as she blinked

rapidly to dispel the image. He's merely playing a part.

There was a need to re-focus her attention, and she glanced idly round the auditorium, catching sight of a familiar face here and there...and found herself trapped in Celine's gaze.

Venom was reflected there. Sheer, unadulterated hatred.

It was as if time hung suspended, and Ana unconsciously held her breath. She lifted a hand to her throat in protective self-defence, then sought to cover the gesture by touching the diamond pendant resting there.

Dear heaven. How could anyone be filled with such malevolence? Or be so possessed by an obsessive emotion that it led towards destruction?

A shiver of apprehension slithered down Ana's spine. Premonition? But what? And where and when?

This was a civilised society, and Celine moved among the echelon of Sydney's wealthy élite. Realistically, what damage could she cause?

It was one thing to be prone to envy and jealousy, but quite another to act on it.

'Ana. Luc. How nice to see you here.'

Ana recognised the feminine voice and entered into conversation with one of the city's society matrons whose untiring support to charity organisations was legendary.

It produced, as it was meant to, an invitation to an upcoming event during the following month.

'You're keeping well, Ana?'

A polite query, or had the woman heard news of her pregnancy? Word flew with the speed of lightning in the social set.

'Fine, thank you.'

She was spared anything further by an announcement over the speaker system advising the guest stars had arrived and would soon be entering the auditorium.

Red carpet, security...light background music. It was all part of the hype and glamour of the evening.

As one, the invited guests turned towards the red carpet waiting for the first VIP to enter, and Ana felt Luc's arms circle her waist as he drew her back against him.

His breath was warm as it fanned her cheek, and she gave in to temptation and leaned in to him, exulting in the way his arms tightened a little.

Held like this, she could almost imagine everything was right in their marriage. That he adored her, and nothing, *no one* could come between them.

To know, irrevocably, the night and every night for the rest of their lives would end with a shared intimacy that was uniquely theirs...

A reverent hush was heard through the auditorium as the first star guest appeared at the head of the red carpet, followed soon after by another.

The female lead was exquisitely dressed, her long

hair beautifully styled, make-up expertly applied, and a figure to die for.

Recent emotional tragedy had marred her life, but it was undetectable in her smile, her soft laughter, the way she crossed from one side of the red carpet to the other as she paused to greet guests who'd come to see her.

As an actress, she was superb, and Ana silently applauded her in admiration for her ability to put her personal life aside in public.

The lead actor followed, and he was charm personified as he worked the room, doing his job for the publicity machine.

The usual entourage appeared, together with the director and producer, then they were through and the invited guests were encouraged to take their seats.

Celine, Ana was relieved to see, was seated three rows to their left, and she felt herself relax as the lights dimmed and the curtain swept open.

Throughout the film she was conscious of Luc's close proximity. The warmth of his hand as he held her own, the shared glance and quiet laughter when a pertinent clip stirred the audience.

The film ran a little over two hours, and there was a collective sigh when the credits began to roll, followed by applause.

It had, Ana admitted, been an entertaining experience, and one she'd enjoyed. She said so as the lights came on, and they joined guests in a slow-moving queue departing the cinema.

Tea, coffee, champagne were being offered in the auditorium, encouraging guests to linger and discuss the film.

Would Celine elect to join them there? It seemed impossible to imagine she wouldn't, and Ana sipped tea as she waited for the moment her nemesis would intrude.

Except the minutes slipped by to become several, and there was no sign of her. Unusual. Definitely unusual. Celine was not one to miss an opportunity!

'Ready to leave?'

Ana caught Luc's quiet drawl, and inclined her head. 'Whenever you are.'

It took a while to slip free and leave the auditorium, for there were acquaintances, friends whom they paused to speak to…but no Celine. Had she already left?

The Mercedes whispered through the city streets, and Ana let her thoughts drift to speculate on Rebekah's date with Jace Dimitriades.

Had it been successful? She fervently hoped so. Tomorrow she'd discover the details…

Luc traversed the New South Head road to suburban Vaucluse, then he turned the car into the sweeping drive leading to their home.

Minutes later they entered the foyer and took the stairs to their suite.

Luc closed the door behind them, then crossed the

room to her side. With infinite care he unclasped the pendant at her nape and placed it on a nearby pedestal, then his hands closed over her shoulders as he turned her round to face him.

Ana was powerless against the softness of his mouth as it caressed her own, his touch an evocative supplication as it teased and tasted in a manner that melted her bones.

His tongue took a low, sweet sweep, tantalising with the promise of what would follow, and she angled her mouth to his, seeking deeper exploration in the prelude to passion.

With evident reluctance he lifted his head and sought the zip fastening of her gown, sliding it free so the soft fabric fell at her feet in a silken heap.

The absence of a bra had proven a provocation all evening, and the thought of freeing her smooth breasts, weighing them in his hands, caressing them with his mouth, the edge of his teeth, had almost driven him wild.

Did she have any idea how heart-stoppingly beautiful she was? Not just in body, but of heart and soul?

So generous and giving, she was part of him, and he sought to show her with his hands, his mouth, exulting in her sultry moan as he took her high, only to emit a husky groan as he helped her tear his clothes free to allow her the same privilege.

Ana loved the taste of his skin, the faint male muskiness, and the light sheen of sensual heat that rose as she trailed her mouth to his shaft and savoured there.

Too soon he dragged her up against him, kissing her deeply as he carefully pulled her onto the bed, and his loving became the sweetest she'd ever known. Power and gentleness. Acute sensuality and hunger. Together they meshed as one in an intoxicating ravishment that was all-consuming. *Mesmeric*.

After-play was inevitably the sweetest, the slow drift of hands, the soft touch of lips…the languor of complete satiation.

Tomorrow he would leave for Melbourne. Three days, two nights. She'd miss him…dreadfully.

CHAPTER TEN

ANA woke late, discovered within minutes that Luc had already left, and tried to stem her feeling of disappointment as she showered, dressed, and prepared for the day ahead.

As always the morning part of the day was the busiest, with processing orders, tying preparation time in with the four scheduled delivery pick-ups.

There were the usual delays and interruptions, and a prospective assistant won their hearts and the job when she offered an immediate start.

'OK, last night, dinner, Jace,' Ana queried during a lull around midday. 'Tell me.' They'd sent the new girl out for a lunch break and an order for sandwiches.

Rebekah seemed strangely hesitant. 'Not what I expected.'

Her eyes narrowed. 'What do you mean…not what you expected?'

'The restaurant was great, the food better than great…' She trailed to a halt, and effected a slight shrug. 'It was just…different.'

'As in?'

'We talked.'

Ana's mouth curved into a musing smile. 'You didn't expect to talk?'

'I mean, discussions, opinions, views.'

'Anything in particular, or just generally?'

'A day in the life of a florist. Anecdotes.'

'And...nothing?'

'No teasing, flirting, or attempt at seduction.'

Jace seemed intent on playing it cool, Ana perceived, and wondered if he would see through her sister's façade, past the hurt and the betrayal to the heart of a woman who had so much love to gift to the right man.

'Are you seeing him again?'

Rebekah chewed the edge of her lip in a gesture of pensive distraction. 'I don't think so.'

I don't think so was an improvement on the definitive *no* her sister would have uttered a few days ago.

Ana chose not to pursue it further, and she turned her attention back to the computer screen.

The phone rang, and she picked up the receiver. 'Blooms and Bouquets, Ana speaking.' The greeting was automatic, her voice warm, friendly and professional.

'I want to place an order if you can guarantee delivery before this afternoon.'

It would be tight, but do-able, and Ana wrote down the relevant details, double-checked the address and keyed it into the computer, took credit-card details, and concluded, 'May I have your name, please?'

'Celine Moore.'

Oh, hell. Celine had never placed a phone order with them before. The question popped into Ana's head...*why now?*

'Problems?'

'Hopefully not.' She bit the edge of her lip, then ran another check on written and computer details to ensure they matched. 'That was Celine.'

Rebekah's eyebrows rose. 'She's ordered flowers?'

'A rushed delivery before noon,' she confirmed. 'Now, why am I suspicious?'

'You think it's a deliberate set-up?'

'I think there's a definite purpose.'

Rebekah crossed to the counter, checked the details, then moved back to the work table. 'I'll do it now.'

Lunch was something Ana ate during a brief break from the computer, and she ignored her sister's admonition with a mischievous grin as she screwed up the paper from her take-away sandwich and tossed it successfully into the wastebin.

'Think you've won, huh?' Rebekah demanded with a teasing laugh. 'Mid-afternoon you get to sip tea at the café and browse through a magazine. *Capisce?*'

Ana wrinkled her nose. 'Since when did you speak Italian?'

'Heard it on television.'

There was a lull around two, then the pace picked

up as Rebekah readied orders for the afternoon delivery.

The door buzzer sounded, followed by Rebekah's softly voiced curse, and Ana glanced up from the computer screen to check the cause, then immediately wished she hadn't, for there was Celine in a whirl of indignant volubility bearing down on her.

Rebekah stepped forward to intercept the woman's progress, only for Celine to bypass her and continue to where Ana sat behind the counter.

'Is there a problem, Celine?'

'Would I be here, if there wasn't?'

'Perhaps you could be specific?'

The divorcee drew herself up to her full height and assumed an expression of hauteur. 'I ordered a delivery of flowers this morning. They haven't reached the person for whom they were intended. I specified same-day delivery and paid the extra cost to have them there prior to midday.'

Ana called up the order on computer, then she checked the order book…a double system to minimise an error in recording apartment and private house numbers.

She scrolled through the day's listing…there it was. 'Apartment 7, 5 Wilson Place.' She named the suburb.

'No, no. It was apartment 5, 7 Wilson Place.'

Aware how easy it was to transpose numbers, Ana took particular care ensuring she got them right, repeating the numbers and writing them down, then requesting the customer to repeat them again as she keyed them into the computer. It wasn't a totally infallible system, but it came close.

'I don't believe I made a mistake,' she said quietly, and saw the angry glitter in Celine's eyes intensify.

'*You* made the error, you're liable. What's more, I've cancelled my credit-card purchase details.'

'I'll check with the delivery firm, and have him double-check his delivery details.'

Celine began tapping the tips of her elegantly polished nails against the counter top. 'Get on to it, Ana. I'm not moving from here until this mess is sorted out.'

Ana used speed-dial, accessed the courier, explained the problem, and held while he checked his records. Minutes later she had the address confirmed, and she ended the call.

'The order was delivered to the address you gave me. Apartment 7, 5 Wilson Place.'

'I refuse to place any further orders with you.' Celine's voice rose, deliberately, Ana suspected, to ensure the two customers who had just entered the shop could hear. 'This is the second time in a week you managed to stuff something up.'

As an actress, she was superb, Ana conceded. Total melodrama, right down to the hand gestures, the tone, the body language. She had to still the desire to applaud her performance.

'That's your choice, Celine.' On her way home,

she'd do a little investigation of her own and visit both apartments. If only to satisfy herself Celine was bent on creating deliberate mischief.

'You haven't heard the last of this,' Celine declared haughtily, and she swept from the shop in a blaze of triumph as the two customers hastily replaced two prepared bouquets and followed suit.

Rebekah released a pent-up sigh. 'Charming.'

'Surely you jest?' The query held uncustomary cynicism.

'With friends like Celine, who needs enemies? More pertinent, what are we going to do about her?'

'I have an idea in mind.' She relayed it, and Rebekah grinned in response.

'We'll both reconnoitre the scene, then go on somewhere for dinner and catch a movie.'

'Done.'

It was after six when they managed to lock up, and a short while later they entered Wilson Place, parked, then entered the apartment building.

They called the manager, explained the situation, and proceeded through to the bank of lifts.

The occupant of Apartment 7 *had* received an unexpected delivery of flowers and figured to keep them.

Alerting the florist listed on the accompanying card of the error wasn't an option the occupant considered.

It was a case of exiting the building and crossing to the adjoining building where they repeated the process, and discovered apartment 5 was owned by a Celine Moore.

'Bingo.'

'Are you thinking what I'm thinking?' Rebekah asked quizzically as they retraced their steps to the car.

'Subterfuge and sabotage?'

'Oh, I'd say there's a very good chance…like one hundred per cent.'

Ana slid in behind the wheel and slid the key into the ignition. 'So…what do you think we should do about it?'

'Confrontation, definitely.'

'You, or me?'

Rebekah's gaze held a purposeful gleam. 'Oh, allow me.'

'You will employ subtlety.'

'Like hell. No one plays a game like this one and gets away with it.'

'OK, let's go home, hit the shower, then go eat.'

They did, and incurred Petros's long-suffering expression. 'I prepared dinner, Ms Dimitriades.'

'Ana,' she corrected from habit. 'And I told you at breakfast we'd probably eat out.'

'You didn't ring and confirm.'

She'd meant to, she really had. 'I'm sorry. I hope you didn't go to a lot of trouble?'

'Apricot chicken with rice, steamed vegetables, and a lemon soufflé.'

It made pizza eaten alfresco sound positively peasant-style in comparison.

Ana turned to her sister and arched an eyebrow. 'Want to eat in, or out? Your choice.'

'Have you had your dinner, Petros?' Rebekah asked, and the manservant shook his head.

'Not yet. I intended to serve you both first.'

'Then you must eat ours instead. We're going up to the Cross to get pizza.'

Petros gave a good imitation of being totally scandalised. 'King's Cross?'

'The same.'

'I must urge you very strongly against going there. Luc would not approve.'

Ana wrinkled her nose at him. 'Luc isn't here.'

'He'll find out.'

'Only if you tell him.'

'It's really most inadvisable.'

'There are two of us, we're only going to eat pizza, then drive on to the cinema complex. What can happen?'

'At least let me drive you.'

'We promise not to park in a side-street, and we both have cellphones,' Ana relayed. 'Trust me, at the first hint of trouble you'll be the first person we call.'

'There are any number of places in which to eat pizza. Why the Cross?'

'Because,' Rebekah said carefully. 'I have a friend who works there, and he makes the best pizza I've ever tasted.'

Petros was clearly torn, and Ana almost felt sorry for him. 'We'll be fine. I'll ring when we're done and on our way to the cinema.'

'Thank you.'

'Anyone,' Rebekah declared with a touch of exasperation as they cleared the driveway, 'would think he had adopted a paternal role.'

'He's answerable to Luc,' Ana said simply.

'Who is an exceedingly wealthy man.' She cast her sister a rueful glance. 'Protective, possessive...or just plain cautious?'

Possessive? 'He's involved in huge money deals.'

'And protective of his pregnant wife.'

'Who is responsible for a Dimitriades heir.'

'That was way too cynical. Why?'

They reached Rose Bay, and took the circuitous route towards Double Bay. 'Blame it on hormones and a preoccupation with Celine's latest contretemps.'

'You think it's aimed at gaining Luc's attention?'

'Without doubt.'

Rebekah pulled up at a set of traffic lights. 'Luc is a hunk.'

'*Thanks.*'

Rebekah laughed, shifted gears, then eased the car forward as the lights went to green. 'Like, you're worried?'

Ana didn't answer, and Rebekah swore briefly. 'Dammit, you *are* worried. Has he given you a reason to be?'

She hesitated a second too long. 'Not really.'

'Don't you trust him?'

Oh, God. Did she? *Completely?* 'I don't trust Celine.' Wasn't that the truth!

'You didn't answer my question.'

Rushcutter's Bay was in the foreground, and any time soon they'd reach the Cross.

'They once shared a relationship.'

'So?' Rebekah released a sound that was akin to a snort. 'I was once married to a man, whom if I never see him again, it would be too soon!'

'That doesn't add up.'

'The hell it doesn't.'

The El Alamein fountain came into sight, and Rebekah's attention became focused on finding a space to park the car. Not easy at the Cross, and Ana was relieved at the distraction.

At this time of evening with daylight beginning to fade, the main street held a mix of people of various cultures whose mode of attire ranged from the norm to the bizarre.

Men in fashionable suits, flashing an over-indulgence of jewellery, looked a little too slick and polished to be ordinary businessmen. Professionals, certainly, but *ordinary*…not.

Then there were the flamboyant types, whose mode of dress bordered on the outrageous, sporting a range of body piercing that almost defied description.

The pizzeria was situated on the main street, and

Rebekah led Ana indoors, greeted the head pizza-maker, then found a table close to the window.

Oven-fired, delectable, mouth-watering aromas filled the small room, and Ana consulted the menu, Rebekah, then placed an order for a large combination pizza to share.

Declining wine or coffee, she settled for tea while Rebekah chose strong espresso.

It was interesting to watch the street scene, to see the people who came to observe and those who came to work. Touts stood in front of doorways outlined in flashing lights, bright neon, cajoling the passersby to come inside and be entertained by strip-shows, nude showgirls.

As the evening crept on, there would be the pimps, the prostitutes, and a steady parade of vehicles dropping off the girls, picking them up. There was more use per square mile of cellphones at the Cross than anywhere else in the city.

That was the visible. The invisible was the existence of a darker world, backstreets where drug deals and less than salubrious activities were done.

Their pizza was served, and after one bite Ana had to agree the taste was out of this world. Ambrosia.

'Has Luc given you reason to distrust him?'

Rebekah had the tenacity of a terrier unwilling to give up a bone, and Ana closed her eyes in exasperation, then quickly opened them again.

She shrugged her shoulders in a gesture of eloquent indecision. 'He flies interstate regularly on business, overseas...New York, London, Paris, Athens. How would I know if anyone joined him there?'

Rebekah's expression became thoughtful. 'Luc cares for you.'

Ana took another slice of pizza and bit into it.

'If it weren't for the child—'

'Oh, *rubbish*. Think about it! He gave you space on the Coast before hauling you home. He could easily have had Dad charged...but he didn't. He's given Celine the flick in no uncertain terms.' She paused for breath. 'Get real. The man adores you!' She leaned forward and covered her sister's hand with her own. 'Besides, he's not the type to play around.'

'Easy to say.'

Rebekah eased back in her chair. 'I think I'm going to hit you. In fact, I'm darned sure of it!'

Sisterhood was a wonderful thing. Ana summoned a smile. 'I'll return the favour if ever our positions are reversed, and Jace Dimitriades gets the better of you!'

'That's a favour going wanting,' Rebekah assured with alacrity.

It was after eight when they entered the cinema complex, and the movie had a feel-good plot, with light-hearted humour and great acting. They emerged at the end of the session, walked to the car, then drove home to sit sipping hot chocolate as they recounted amusing aspects of the film.

There was a text message from Luc on Ana's cellphone, which she chose to ignore. Received while she was in the cinema, it was brief to the point of abruptness.

If he wanted to speak to her, he could ring again.

He did, just as she slipped into bed.

'You didn't return my call.'

'Well, hello to you, too,' she responded with pseudo-politeness.

'I didn't wake you?'

She almost made a facetious reply, then thought better of it. 'No.'

'I rang earlier. Petros said you were out.'

'Eating pizza at the Cross, then taking in a movie.'

She could almost feel the silence weighing in from the other end of the line. 'If that's a joke, it's a bad one.'

'Rebekah has a friend who makes the most divine pizza.'

'At the Cross,' he chided with chilling softness.

She was beginning to enjoy this. 'Uh-huh.'

'I trust you won't be going there again?'

'We might.'

'You're having fun with this, aren't you?'

Her smile was deliciously wicked. 'Oh, yes.'

'Just remember I'll be home day after tomorrow,' Luc declared silkily. 'Will you be so brave then?'

'Of course. You don't frighten me in the least.'

'Careful, *pedhaki mou*.'

'Always. Goodnight.' She ended the call and switched off the phone.

CHAPTER ELEVEN

'DANGER at twenty paces,' Rebekah warned, *sotto voce*.

Ana glanced up and saw Celine bearing down on her. Here we go again, she accorded silently. The witch from Rose Bay.

'I suppose you think you're clever.'

'Another problem, Celine?'

The woman's eyes glittered with anger. 'What right do you have to check up on your customers?'

'Any complaint regarding delivery is always investigated,' Ana said smoothly. 'You accused Blooms and Bouquets of making an error and rescinded payment of your account.'

'That allows you to badger people?'

There was no doubt this was going to get nasty. 'Badger, Celine? My sister and I checked both apartment addresses personally. The lady at apartment 7, 5 Wilson Place confirmed she'd received a delivery not meant for her. We were able to ascertain apartment 5, 7 Wilson Place is owned by you.'

'What nonsense. Why would I send flowers to a vacant apartment?'

'Why, indeed?'

Celine's features became a study in white fury. 'Are you accusing me of foul play?'

Ana had had enough. 'Your words, Celine. Not mine.'

She didn't see it coming, and it happened so unexpectedly, so quickly, there was no time for evasive action.

In one swift movement Celine swept a large glass vase off the counter.

It knocked against Ana's arm, sending a shower of water over her thighs, and shattered on impact with the concrete floor, sending shards of glass in all directions.

What came next was unbelievable, and she gasped out loud as Celine shoved her so hard she lost her balance, skidded on the wet floor, and went down in seemingly slow motion.

'You *bitch*,' Rebekah hissed angrily, and Ana registered the sound of a palm connecting with flesh.

The next instant Rebekah hunkered down, her face pale as she checked for injuries.

Ana raised stunned eyes, then followed her sister's gaze. There was glass everywhere, blood streamed from a gash on her arm, another on her leg, her hand where she'd attempted to soften her fall.

'Stay there,' Rebekah instructed. 'Don't move. I'm ringing the ambulance.'

Oh, dear God…the fall…could she miscarry? No, surely not. It hadn't been a hard fall. 'An ambulance is definite overkill. It's only a few cuts. Get some paper towels, and I'll clean myself up.' Initial surprise had begun to wane, and in its place was shocked disbelief.

'Petros, then.' Rebekah was already dialling, and seconds later she spoke rapidly, then replaced the receiver. 'He's leaving immediately. Now, let's get you into a chair, then I'll attempt to clean up this mess. But first,' she said with angry determination, 'I get to take a photo to use as evidence.'

'You're kidding me, right?'

'No.'

It took only brief seconds, then she caught hold of Rebekah's outstretched hands and stepped gingerly over to the chair. Broken glass crunched beneath her shoes, and she stood still as her sister brushed glass from her clothes.

'Are you OK?'

It hadn't been a heavy fall, and she said so. 'Apart from a few cuts, yes.'

'Sit down, and stay there while I get rid of all this.' She plucked disposable towelling into sheets and carefully stemmed the flow of blood.

Minutes later the glass was swept into a dustpan, and the vacuum cleaner sucked up any remaining splinters. A few swirls with the mop to remove the water puddles and everything was restored to normal.

Petros appeared soon after, and Ana registered he must have broken the speed limit to arrive so quickly. He took one look, and his eyes went black with anger.

'I'll take you to the hospital.'

'Home, Petros. It's only a few scratches.'

'The hospital, Ana,' he reiterated firmly. Without pausing, he scooped her into his arms, ignored her protest, and spoke to Rebekah over his shoulder as he walked towards the door. 'I'll ring as soon as the doctor has attended to her.'

It was, she registered with amusement, the first time he'd used her Christian name. Later, she'd tease him about it. But for now she was content to have him take charge.

The Mercedes was double-parked at the kerb, the passenger door open, and he lowered her into the seat.

'Petros, I didn't know you cared.' Flippancy was the only way to go, and she glimpsed a muscle clench at the edge of his jaw before he straightened and moved round the car to take the wheel.

The hospital staff were efficient. Excruciatingly so. Petros hovered, then retreated, only to reappear minutes later.

Two gashes required sutures. They examined her from top to toe, did an ultrasound, admitted her for observation, and the obstetrician conducted an examination.

Petros stood guard in the room, and only left it on instruction from the sister-in-charge.

'You're fine, my dear.' The obstetrician reassured, 'The baby is fine. No sign of foetal distress.'

'I can go home?'

'Tomorrow.' He offered a faint smile. 'We'll keep you in overnight as a precaution.'

Why did she get the feeling this was a conspiracy?

As soon as he left she rang the shop, spoke to Rebekah, then she settled back against the cushions and reflected on Celine's actions, retracing to the moment the woman entered the shop.

Had Celine meant to cause deliberate harm? Or was it merely a heat-of-the-moment thing? It was difficult to judge.

A nurse brought in tea and a few courtesy magazines, followed soon after by the sister-in-charge, who queried her level of comfort.

Lunch came and went, and reaction must have taken its toll, for she woke from a light doze to find Luc seated in the chair beside her bed.

'What are you doing here?'

He rose to his feet and moved to her side. His faint smile held warmth, but there was something evident in his eyes she didn't care to define.

'Is that any way to greet your husband?' He lowered his head and closed his mouth over hers in a light, evocative kiss, lingered, then he took it deeper in a desperate need to feel her response.

Did she have any idea what he'd gone through in the last few hours? Petros's call had shattered him, totally, then cold, hard anger set in as he swiftly organised his return to Sydney. Something that was achieved within minutes, then he'd simply walked out of a meeting, taken the car one of his colleagues immediately made available, and headed to the airport.

He made a few calls from his cellphone, called in favours, enlisted the services of the city's top obstetrician, checked with the hospital, then he rang Celine.

His eyes hardened as he recalled her sickening coquetry, the shocked surprise, followed by consternation over the accusations he levelled at her. Then, when he left her in no doubt as to his intended action, there was anger and vitriol.

The hour's flight had seemed like an eternity, and he'd instructed Petros to sit on the speed limit between the airport and hospital.

He already had the obstetrician's report, but he desperately needed visual reassurance.

No one had halted his passage through Reception, nor did anyone query his presence as he bypassed the lift and took the stairs. At the first-floor nursing station the sister-in-charge opened her mouth in protest, then quickly closed it again as she witnessed the grim determination evident.

He didn't pause when he reached Ana's suite, and simply pushed open the door with clear disregard for a courtesy knock. And came to a halt at the sight of her propped against a bank of pillows.

Her head was turned slightly to one side, and her eyes were closed in sleep.

For a long moment he just stood there, drinking in her features in repose. It took tremendous will-power to restrain himself from crossing to the bed and lifting her into his arms.

He almost did, and would have if he thought the movement wouldn't hurt her.

Instead, he'd settled himself in the chair and waited for her to wake.

'Hmm,' Ana murmured as his mouth left hers and trailed up to brush against her temple. 'Nice.'

She could almost sense his smile, and a slow warmth heated her skin. This close she could breathe in the scent of him, the subtle cologne meshing with a male muskiness that was his alone.

He brushed his lips across her forehead, lingered, then pressed one eyelid closed before slipping down to the edge of her mouth.

She angled her head a little and parted her lips against his own in a kiss that promised, but didn't take as it became frankly sensual, tasting, probing, then easing back to graze a little.

When at last he lifted his head she could only look at him in bemusement. 'Maybe I should become a hospital patient more often.'

'Not if I can help it.'

He looked gorgeous, so intensely male, so much a part of her. It seemed important to endorse the obstetrician's reassurance. 'The baby's fine.'

Luc lifted a hand and brushed light fingers across her cheek. 'What about *you, agape mou*?' His hand moved to cup her chin, tilting it a little. 'Want to tell me what happened this morning?'

Her gaze held his, clear and unblinking. 'It's over.'

'Yes. It is.' He traced the pad of one finger over her lower lip.

'I have no doubt Petros has relayed his version.'

'Indeed.' He felt her mouth tremble, and his eyes darkened. 'Rebekah, also.' His hand slid round to cup her nape, gently massaging the back of her neck and into the base of her skull. 'I can promise Celine will never get close to you again.'

It must be reaction, but there was something happening here...something deep and meaningful. Except it was just out of reach, and she couldn't quite grasp hold of it.

He cared, without doubt. But was it merely fondness for someone he held in affectionate regard?

'You're the one she wants,' Ana said simply. 'And I'm in the way.'

'The only one in the way is Celine.' His voice held a dangerous quality.

The door swished open and a nurse collected the chart, then crossed to the bed to take Ana's vital signs. Minutes later they were punctiliously recorded, and she left the suite to continue her round.

'Is there anything you need?'

Oh, my, how did she answer that? She lifted a hand, then dropped it again, and shook her head. 'Petros packed a few things and brought them in.' She offered him a winsome smile. 'He called me *Ana* for the first time ever.'

'Quite an achievement.' He skimmed a hand over her shoulder. 'Are you in any pain?'

Not the physical kind. No matter how she attempted to understand Celine's driven action, a lingering shock remained. She wasn't concerned for herself, but her unborn child was something else.

She closed her eyes in the hope she could also close her mind to the woman's vicious jealousy-motivated action.

'Go home, Luc,' she bade quietly.

'Not a chance.' He crossed to the chair and folded his length into it.

When next Ana looked he was still there, and she shook her head in silent remonstrance. Nursing staff came and went with monotonous regularity, and the arrival of the dinner trolley with an extra meal for Luc brought a further protest.

'There's no need for you to stay.'

'Indulge me.'

This was too much. He was too much. 'I haven't heard your cellphone ring once.'

'It's turned off.'

The in-room television provided visual entertainment, and Luc finally conceded to leave long after visiting hours were over.

Ana was unaware of the private security guard posted in the corridor out of her sight, or that Luc had the nursing station on alert.

It was undoubtedly over the top, but he didn't give

a damn. No one toyed with him or one of his own without paying the price.

He reached his car, slid in behind the wheel, and eased it out from the hospital car park. There were other issues that were long overdue. Way overdue, he amended grimly.

First, he'd reorganise his business interests and take Ana to the beach house on the Central Coast.

Petros was hovering inside the door when Luc entered the house. 'Ms Ana is well?'

'Yes, thank God. She'll be home tomorrow.'

'Nasty business.'

Luc shot the older man a level glance. 'It's been taken care of.'

'One would hope so.'

There was no need for further words. Luc's influence was a known entity. As an enemy, he was deadly.

A slight smile tugged the edges of Luc's mouth. 'She told me you called her *Ana*.' One eyebrow slanted. 'Quite a departure from your usual formality.'

'I shall see it doesn't happen again.'

'I imagine she'll never let you forget it.'

Petros allowed himself a warm smile. 'No, I don't suppose she will.'

CHAPTER TWELVE

THE new day's dawn brought a sense of new beginnings, and Ana rose early, showered and dressed, then participated in the morning's hospital routine. The obstetrician called in, she ate a healthy breakfast, then she dealt with the discharge process prior to Luc's arrival at nine to take her home.

Petros emerged from the front door as Luc's Mercedes drew to a halt beneath the wide portico, and he opened the passenger door as Luc slid out from behind the wheel.

'It's good to have you home, Ms—'

'*Ana,*' she interrupted firmly, the glint in her eyes fearsome. 'If you dare call me anything else, I'll *hit* you.'

'Very well.'

She looked at him in silent askance.

'Ms—'

'Just…Ana,' she said gently.

'You've lost that particular skirmish,' Luc declared as he preceded Petros indoors, and the older man hid a faint smile.

'So it would appear.'

'Everything is in order?'

Petros inclined his head. 'All that remains is for Ana to pack a bag.'

She paused mid-stride at the foot of the stairs. 'What do you mean, *pack*?'

Luc curved an arm along the back of her waist and urged her towards the upper floor. 'We're spending a few days at the beach house.'

'Don't you have to go into the office?'

'The world won't stop if I'm not there.'

No, it wouldn't. But Luc was a man who kept a constant eye on the business ball.

They reached the bedroom, and she surveyed the large suite, appreciating its familiarity. Two bags reposed on the long stand at the foot of the bed. One closed, the other empty. His laptop rested on the floor.

Luc turned her into his arms and lowered his head down to hers. His mouth was incredibly gentle as it brushed her own, and she linked both hands at his nape to hold him there as she deepened the kiss.

His hands shifted, one slipping down to cup her bottom while the other slid up to fist her hair.

Dear heaven, she needed this. The feel of him, his touch, his male scent, and the warmth and heat of his embrace.

A faint groan rose and died in her throat as he trailed a path along the edge of her jaw to linger close to the sensitive hollow beneath her earlobe, then he followed the cord at the edge of her neck and nuzzled there before slipping down to savour the delicate arch of her throat.

With obvious reluctance he eased back and pressed a light kiss to the edge of her mouth. His heart beat in tune with her own, heavy and fast.

'Go pack, *pedhi mou*. Otherwise we won't be heading anywhere soon.'

It didn't help that he was right, although she conceded they had time ahead of them. Consequently she slipped out of his arms and collected a few clothes together, then she followed Luc down to the car.

In less than an hour they reached the beach house. Although *beach house* was hardly an adequate description for the delightful double-storeyed home built only metres from the sandy foreshore. The external walls comprised tempered tinted glass, and palm trees and shrubbery lent privacy whilst providing tranquil views out over the ocean.

Petros had rung ahead, for there were provisions in the pantry, fresh milk and juice in the refrigerator, and the house was spotlessly clean.

Ana crossed the lounge and stood close to the huge expanse of glass, drinking in the deep blue waters of the Pacific Ocean, clear today of any craft. She could almost smell the salt-spray and feel the crunch of sand beneath her feet.

'Feel like a walk along the beach?'

She turned and took hold of Luc's outstretched hand, then together they left the house and took the short path through the palm trees and planted shrubbery to the bank of white sand leading down to the water.

It was a beautiful day, warm with brilliant sunshine and hardly a cloud in the sky.

The gently curved cove appeared isolated, and Ana had the uncanny feeling they could have been alone in the world.

They strolled down to where the sand was packed and damp from an outgoing tide, then they followed the tide-line towards an outcrop of rocks in the distance.

There were questions she wanted to ask, but she was hesitant to begin, and unsure if his answers would be what she wanted to hear.

So much had happened in the past few months. So many misunderstandings and misconceptions. Untruths and false accusations.

One could never go back, she reflected sadly, or undo the things said and done. There was only one direction, and that was forward. Yet some things in the past could affect the future if they weren't confronted and resolved. For only then was it possible to move on.

And one of those things in the immediate past was Celine.

Perhaps she could begin there.

'Did Celine mean anything to you?' Nothing like taking the bull by the horns!

Luc stopped walking and turned towards her. His

eyes were dark, and she could almost sense the latent anger that simmered beneath the surface of his control.

'No. We shared a brief relationship several years ago,' he reiterated quietly. 'She wanted marriage, I didn't. I moved on, and she married someone else.'

'Yet you continued to see each other,' Ana pursued, and glimpsed a muscle tense at the edge of his jaw.

'We lived in the same city, moved in the same social circle.' His expression assumed wry cynicism. 'We observed a state of polite civility.'

'Until her divorce.'

He slid his hands up her arms to cradle her shoulders. 'After her divorce,' he corrected. 'Why would I want to have anything to do with another woman, when I have *you*?'

Something stirred deep inside and began to unfurl. Hope. Dared she begin to *hope*?

'She embarked on a relentless campaign,' Ana ventured, holding his gaze.

'I've initiated legal action against her.' His hands slid up to cup her face. 'She'll pay, and pay dearly. If she has any sense, she'll relocate to another city. Preferably another country.'

As an enemy, he was ruthless. 'I see.'

'Do you, Ana?' His eyes searched hers, dark with passion and another emotion she couldn't define.

'Emma—'

He placed a finger to her lips, closing them.

'Emma was my youth,' he said gently. 'I mourned her loss. Not so much for myself, but for the too short a time she spent on this earth.' His mouth curved into a warm smile. 'She was sunshine, laughter, and she was my best friend.' He traced the outline of her lower lip. 'But she could never be *you*.'

She felt her bones begin to melt, and her eyes seemed to ache with suppressed emotion.

'You stole my heart, and captured my soul.'

She almost swayed on her feet. Was he saying he *loved* her?

'Luc—'

He didn't let her finish. 'You're my life, my love. Everything.'

Her eyes shimmered with unshed tears, and she blinked rapidly to stem their flow. Except one spilled over and trickled slowly down her cheek.

He followed the trail with the pad of his thumb, and his smile was almost her undoing.

'How could you not know, *agape mou*? Each time I held you in my arms, whenever we made love? Didn't you feel it in the beat of my heart, my touch?'

Oh, God, she was going to cry. 'You never said the words.'

'I'm going to have to teach you Greek.'

'I thought—'

He gave her a gentle shake. 'I married you for the convenience of having a woman in my bed, a social hostess?' His eyes became dark. 'If that's all I wanted, I would have remarried years ago.'

She opened her mouth, then closed it again.

'I love you, Ana. *Love*. The *till death us do part* kind. Without you, I wouldn't want to live.'

She wasn't capable of saying a word. All this time she'd thought affection was the foundation of their marriage. Now she was filled with a wondrous disbelief.

'Celine worked her poison with diabolical success,' Luc continued. 'Worse, you chose to believe her, and nothing I said seemed to convince you otherwise.'

Diabolical success? Yes, it had been that. Celine had known which buttons to push and how to screw each one of them down.

'When you left for the Coast, I thought a few days might help you reflect and gain some perspective. Instead, it merely worked against me.'

He shaped her cheek, and let his thumb slip down to linger at the edge of her mouth. 'Do you have any idea how terrified I was of losing you?'

Her lips parted, but anything she might have said remained locked in her throat.

'Or how I felt when I discovered you were pregnant with our child?'

'You used emotional blackmail.'

'It was the only weapon I had.'

'You wanted the child—'

'I wanted *you*.' He brought her close and tilted her chin. 'Sweet Ana. Our child is a wonderful bonus, a joy I rejoice in because it represents *life*. Yours, mine, *ours*. But make no mistake. *You* are my reason for living. My heart. My soul.'

She reached up and pulled his head down to hers.

'I love you. I always have. Always will. For the rest of my life.'

Then she kissed him, deeply, emotively with great passion, and it was a while before they broke apart to draw breath.

'How dedicated are you to walking along the beach?'

Her eyes held an impish twinkle that matched the laughter in her voice, and he chose to humour her.

'Do you have a better idea?'

She held up her hand and began counting options off on her fingers. 'We could walk, and talk some more. Move up onto dry sand, sit down, admire the ocean view and reflect on the spirituality of *being*. We could engage in a discussion about how much longer I'm going to work.'

'You know how I feel about you working.'

Her eyes were large pools of brilliant sapphire, and deep enough for a man to drown in. And he was beginning to sink...

'Please.' She threaded her fingers through his own, and brought them to her lips. 'Mornings.'

'Three days a week.'

'Four,' Ana amended.

'For another two months,' he conceded.

'Three.'

He slid his hands up to cup her face. 'What in hell am I going to do with you, woman?'

'Love me,' she said solemnly. 'You do it very well.'

'What hope will I have if we produce a blonde-haired, blue-eyed little imp…your image in miniature?' he groaned, bringing his mouth down to hers.

'She'll twist you round her little finger at the first blink of an eye.' She offered him a delighted smile. 'And you'll become her devoted slave for life.'

'Without doubt.' The thought of holding their child for the first time almost brought him undone.

'Of course, it could be a boy…' A dark-haired babe who'd grow tall and strong like his father. She felt quite misty-eyed at the image.

'Are we all talked out yet?' Luc teased as he curved an arm over her shoulders.

'We could go back to the house…'

'I guess that's an option,' he acceded indolently, loving the soft chuckle that escaped her lips.

'And indulge each other?' Ana pretended to consider. 'Now, there's the thing. It's not even lunch-time.'

He took pleasure in watching her play the game. 'Do you have a specific time in mind?'

'Well,' she began carefully, 'given that I'm slightly incapacitated,' she indicated the dressing on one forearm, and her bandaged hand, 'it would mean you'll have to do most of the work. Perhaps you might like to rest first?'

'Minx.'

'Of course, the foreplay needn't be too...' she trailed to a delicate pause '...energetic.'

His deep, throaty laughter startled a resting gull, and it flew into the air uttering a shrill squawk before circling towards the rocky outcrop.

'Let's just see whose energy is depleted first, hmm?' He swept an arm beneath her knees and lifted her high against his chest.

'Put me down.' A delicious chuckle found voice. 'What if someone is watching? Whatever will they think?'

'That we're two people very much in love.'

And they'd be right. Thank God. 'Then it's OK.' She pressed a kiss to his temple. 'But please put me down.' Her eyes were level with his own, and for a moment it seemed as if they each caught a glimpse into each other's soul. 'I want you to conserve your energy.'

Her smile melted his heart. 'And you're doubtful I will, if I carry you back to the house?'

'Well, I wouldn't want you to be diminished in any way.'

Luc let her slip carefully onto her feet, then he looped an arm around her shoulders. 'Home, *agape mou*. I need to hold you, touch, make love to you.'

She turned her head to look at him as they began retracing their steps. 'Ditto.'

It had been, Ana reflected much later as the sun sank down below the horizon, the most perfect day.

Luc stood behind her, his arms curved round her waist, and she leaned back against him, exulting in the feel of his lips as he sought the sensitive hollow at the edge of her neck.

'Beautiful.'

He wasn't referring to the view beyond the wall of glass, but the woman he held so close to his heart.

His wife, the love of his life.

Harlequin is proud to have published
more than 75 novels by

Emma Darcy

Award-
winning Australian
author **Emma Darcy** is a
unique voice in Harlequin
Presents®. Her compelling, sexy,
intensely emotional novels have
gripped the imagination of readers
around the globe, and she's sold
nearly 60 million books
worldwide.

Praise for Emma Darcy:

"Emma Darcy delivers a spicy love story…a fiery conflict
and a hot sensuality."

"Emma Darcy creates a strong emotional premise
and a sizzling sensuality."

"Emma Darcy pulls no punches."

"With exciting scenes, vibrant characters and a layered story line,
Emma Darcy dishes up a spicy reading experience."

—*Romantic Times Magazine*

**Look out for more thrilling stories by Emma Darcy,
coming soon in**

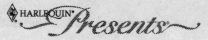

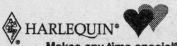

International bestselling author

SANDRA MARTON

invites you to attend the

WEDDING *of the* YEAR

Glitz and glamour prevail in this volume
containing a trio of stories in which
three couples meet at a
high society wedding—and
soon find themselves
walking down the aisle!

Look for it in November 2002.

HARLEQUIN®
Makes any time special®

$\mathscr{F}$ALL IN $\mathscr{L}$OVE
THIS WINTER
WITH
HARLEQUIN BOOKS!

In October 2002 look for these special volumes
led by *USA TODAY* bestselling authors,
and receive a MOULIN ROUGE VHS video*!
*Retail value of $14.99 U.S.

See inside books for details.

**This exciting promotion
is available at your
favorite retail outlet.**

Only from

HARLEQUIN®
Makes any time special®

Visit Harlequin at www.eHarlequin.com   PHNCP02

Princes...Princesses...
London Castles...New York Mansions...
To live the life of a royal!

In 2002, Harlequin Books lets you escape to a
world of royalty with these royally themed titles:

Temptation:
January 2002—*A Prince of a Guy* (#861)
February 2002—*A Noble Pursuit* (#865)

American Romance:
The Carradignes: American Royalty (Editorially linked series)
March 2002—*The Improperly Pregnant Princess* (#913)
April 2002—*The Unlawfully Wedded Princess* (#917)
May 2002—*The Simply Scandalous Princess* (#921)
November 2002—*The Inconveniently Engaged Prince* (#945)

Intrigue:
The Carradignes: A Royal Mystery (Editorially linked series)
June 2002—*The Duke's Covert Mission* (#666)

Chicago Confidential
September 2002—*Prince Under Cover* (#678)

The Crown Affair
October 2002—*Royal Target* (#682)
November 2002—*Royal Ransom* (#686)
December 2002—*Royal Pursuit* (#690)

Harlequin Romance:
June 2002—*His Majesty's Marriage* (#3703)
July 2002—*The Prince's Proposal* (#3709)

Harlequin Presents:
August 2002—*Society Weddings* (#2268)
September 2002—*The Prince's Pleasure* (#2274)

Duets:
September 2002—*Once Upon a Tiara/Henry Ever After* (#83)
October 2002—*Natalia's Story/Andrea's Story* (#85)

Celebrate a year of royalty with
Harlequin Books!

Available at your favorite retail outlet.

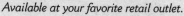

HARLEQUIN®
Makes any time special ®

Visit us at www.eHarlequin.com

HSROY02

Lindsay Armstrong...
Helen Bianchin...
Emma Darcy...
Miranda Lee...

Some of our bestselling writers are Australians!

Look our for their novels about the Wonder from Down Under—where spirited women win the hearts of Australia's most eligible men.

Coming soon:

THE MARRIAGE RISK
by Emma Darcy
On sale February 2001, Harlequin Presents® #2157

And look out for:

MARRIAGE AT A PRICE
by Miranda Lee
On sale June 2001, Harlequin Presents® #2181

Available wherever Harlequin books are sold.

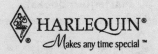